PEN

The T...

Frank Finnigan

Rebekah Palmer, 32, is a first-time novelist, although she has been writing fiction for many years.

She has a BA from Victoria University and a Postgraduate Diploma in Journalism from Canterbury University. An award-winning journalist, she has travelled and worked in Britain, Europe and Asia. She spent seven years with the New Zealand Press Association and now works as a freelance journalist, editor and writer.

Rebekah lives in Wellington with her partner Bernard Steeds and their brand new baby daughter.

The Thirteenth Life of Frank Finnigan

Rebekah Palmer

[signature]

PENGUIN BOOKS

PENGUIN BOOKS
Penguin Books (NZ) Ltd, cnr Airborne and Rosedale Roads, Albany,
Auckland 1310, New Zealand
Penguin Books Ltd, 27 Wrights Lane, London W8 5TZ, England
Penguin Putnam Inc, 375 Hudson Street, New York, NY 10014, United States
Penguin Books Australia Ltd, 487 Maroondah Highway, Ringwood,
Australia 3134
Penguin Books Canada Ltd, 10 Alcorn Avenue, Toronto, Ontario,
Canada M4V 3B2
Penguin Books (South Africa) Pty Ltd, 5 Watkins Street, Denver Ext 4, 2094,
South Africa
Penguin Books India (P) Ltd, 11, Community Centre, Panchsheel Park,
New Delhi 110 017, India

Penguin Books Ltd, Registered Offices: Harmondsworth, Middlesex, England

First published by Penguin Books (NZ) Ltd, 2001

1 3 5 7 9 10 8 6 4 2

Copyright © Rebekah Palmer 2001

The right of Rebekah Palmer to be identified as the author of this work in terms
of section 96 of the Copyright Act 1994 is hereby asserted.

Designed by Mary Egan
Typeset by Egan-Reid Ltd
Printed in Australia by Australian Print Group, Maryborough

All rights reserved. Without limiting the rights under copyright reserved above,
no part of this publication may be reproduced, stored in or introduced
into a retrieval system, or transmitted, in any form or by any means
(electronic, mechanical, photocopying, recording or otherwise), without
the prior written permission of both the copyright owner and
the above publisher of this book.

ISBN 0-14-100454-1

For Bernard

ACKNOWLEDGEMENTS

Grateful thanks to all my friends and family for their support and encouragement.

Thanks to Max Lambert for recounting tales of the *Wahine* disaster and the 'good old days' of journalism, and to Frank Haden for some classic one-liners.

Thanks also to Jane Parkin for her advice and Geoff Walker and Louise Armstrong at Penguin for their enthusiasm.

Prologue

'And so the book begins.'

A sea of applause crashes around the lecture room. Martin joins the other students and rises to his feet, slapping his palms together so hard they ache. Brilliant. The guy is brilliant. Imagine being able to write like that.

The student next to Martin leans over to yell in his ear.

'Now that's real literature. So much for bloody Chaucer!'

'I think I'll do my thesis on him!'

Robertson up front is twitching like a cornered possum. Martin imagines him whispering to Miss Hibbert: 'It may hit the best-seller list but it will never make the canon.'

Miss Hibbert quietens the audience, painting a wall of air with her hands, as if physically pressing the noise levels down.

'Perhaps Mr Finnigan will grant us an encore in light of such a reception. Mr Finnigan?'

Finnigan looks pissed off, but reluctantly rises and returns to the platform.

'I'm not reading any more. You can all go out and bloody well buy it.'

He strides back to his seat as laughter meanders across the auditorium, but Miss Hibbert persists.

'Perhaps we might have a little of something else.'

'You buggers expect a lot for a free appearance.'

But he gets to his feet, grumps over to the microphone, his

beer-belly nudging the lectern, and frowns at the students. Martin searches the shaggy moustache for a hidden smile, finds none.

'I don't normally do this.'

The writer searches through a pocket of his tweed trousers, and the students settle back against the hard wooden seats in anticipation. This is the biggest turn-out all year, the only visiting writer everyone has read, even if they wouldn't all admit it. Martin feels a sense of excitement he hasn't registered since childhood.

'Here it is. I'll read you this, it's a poem I wrote this morning, for my wife.'

'Oh, Frank,' Miss Hibbert begins, before shrinking back under his glare. She looks at her feet like a schoolgirl and Finnigan sniffs, smoothing the scrap of paper against the lectern.

'It's not done yet, but anyway . . .'

And he begins to read, in that gruff voice, devoid of intonation, and Martin has to concentrate to catch the words before they skip into the flooding stream.

> '*He knows he doesn't deserve her.*
> *On days like this it feels like shit,*
> *this secret life,*
> *a bleak unravelling bit by bit.*
> *Still he asks her to inspire,*
> *call him liar.*
> *He cannot tell what's in his heart,*
> *the fears within will not be spilt.*
> *Why then, call it art –*
> *it's a way to expunge the guilt.*
> *And so, he sits and makes a start.*
> *In retribution, or just rage,*
> *He vomits words on to the page.*'

The applause is even louder than before, waves pounding the walls as the writer steps down and shakes the hands of the English lecturers. This time Martin doesn't get to his feet, doesn't even clap, just sits, the phrases still echoing in his ears. This stuff is great. Finnigan would make a great thesis topic.

Belatedly he stands and applauds as the others begin to gather their bags and file into the aisles. A student nudges him: 'Come on mate, I'll be late for philosophy.'

By the blackboard, Martin lingers at the back of a group waiting to talk to Finnigan. Some of them have books for the author to sign: he should have thought of that. He's not sure what he wants to say, just this instinct to make contact. There's something here he's looking for. Finnigan's checking his gold watch, signing books quickly, trying to dismiss the flock of fans. The expensive English tweed he's wearing looks almost like a piss-take.

Standing next to Martin, a tall spotty student stretches an arm forward to grasp the writer's hand.

'Mr Finnigan, I'm in the process of writing my first novel. Do you have any advice?'

Finnigan barely glances at the boy, reaches for another book to sign.

'Write.'

'Sorry?'

Martin registers the note of desperation.

'Just write, kid.'

Martin watches Finnigan's eyes, hooded with heavy lids but bright with intellect. A faint look of amusement lies buried in his jowls. He seems a man with a great weight of experience behind him, as if he's older than his fifty-three years. The salt-sprinkled moustache is huge, bristling over oddly feminine lips.

'That's the only advice I ever have. You want to write, write. Just do it, kid. Don't talk about it, don't dream about it, don't put it off till you know what you're doing, or wait till you know what you want to say, just sit down and *do* it.'

His gaze flits over to Martin, and he looks straight through him.

'Okay, class dismissed.' Miss Hibbert pushes through the

group, hissing and flapping at them. 'Off you go, off you go.'

'Christ, I'd never have made a teacher. I'd have strangled the bastards,' the writer growls.

'Frank, Mr Finnigan, the reading was just wonderful. Please come up to the staffroom before you go, I'm sure my other colleagues would be honoured.'

Martin, deflated, turns to go, unsure of what he's been waiting for.

'Not if they're anything like your Mr Robertson, they won't. No thanks. Hey, kid.'

Martin feels a tap on his shoulder and spins around. The hooded eyes target him, a hawk, a mouse.

'Carry these books out to the car for me, would you?'

'Sure.'

By the time Martin gathers up the assorted books and papers, Finnigan's out the door. Martin hurries after him, leaving Miss Hibbert dithering, rolling a piece of chalk nervously between her fingers. Finnigan's striding towards the street.

'Got to get out of this place,' he calls over his shoulder. 'They lock people up in these ivory towers, don't they? Force you to read things that're good for you. Can't stand bloody universities. All these would-be literati, really they're just a bunch of fuckwits.'

He stops at a breathtaking silvery-blue Jag, parked illegally, and holds open the back door, motioning for Martin to throw in the books.

'Thanks, kid.' He leans close enough for Martin to see inside his nostrils. 'Want some more advice for free?'

Martin just looks at him.

'Get out of here quick, before they get you by the balls.'

And then he's round the other side of the elegant car, getting in and driving off, before Martin has recovered enough to think of anything in reply. He grins stupidly and looks down at the gutter where a small piece of paper is batting against the concrete. The poem. He picks it up and walks away, as guilty as a thief.

Chapter 1

'You will be my Boswell, boy.'

Wellington, July 1996
The weather is straight out of an opening scene from one of Frank's books. Martin looks up at the sky and thinks if he has ever seen clouds as black as a bull's backside, these are them. He laughs quietly as he makes his way down the terracotta-tiled path to the front door. He hopes it's the right address: 58, he's sure it was 58. It must be worth a million dollars – more with the sea views. He nearly trips over a sleek Burmese cat stretched across the foot of the path under the potted rose bushes.

Wake up, there's no need to be nervous.

The house is not as ostentatious as he expected. It is hidden from its neighbours down a bank of bush, very private, you can hardly see it from the road. Its muted earth tones make it blend into the environment. Martin steps up to the huge copper door and rings the bell; it bing-bongs faintly somewhere inside, and he waits, his left hand in his pocket, fingers drumming against his leg. A woman in her late sixties – curly white hair and glasses – heaves on the copper block. She's dressed in a delicate blue, with thick brown stockings and small feet snug in slippers. Incongruously grandmotherish in this modern setting. She smiles shyly, peering like a night animal blinking at the sunshine, and invites him in. She must be the wife.

'I'm Connie. Frank's just through in the sitting room.'

The 'sitting room' is large, with an expanse of plate-glass

windows presenting a dense blue backdrop of sea and sky. The dark clouds make the room feel threatened. Martin looks around, noting the arrangement of furniture: antique French chairs, a couple of lamps, large television, coffee table, lots of bookshelves supporting the side walls, family photos on a dark oak sideboard. No one else is in the room. He fidgets, considers calling Connie who's padding down the hallway; then a figure appears at one of the windows, which turns into a sudden sliding door as the man shoves it aside.

'You're here, then.'

Martin starts forward, hand out, but Finnigan holds his up in surrender, palms covered in dirt.

'Hang on there. Just been killing the wandering jew.'

He goes through to another room, and Martin wonders what the hell he's talking about.

'Come in the kitchen here. I'll get Connie to make us a cuppa, eh, or would you rather a beer? Bit early still, I guess.'

He's at the stainless-steel sink, scrubbing vigorously, the thin slab of soap rapidly blackening.

'Ah, Con. Make us a cup of tea then, would you? Gumboot all right with you, boy?'

'Sorry?'

'Gumboot tea?'

'Oh, yes, sure.'

'Do you take milk, Mr Wrightson?'

She has a slight accent. Martin can't place it – something East European.

'Yes, thank you, Mrs Finnigan.'

'Connie, call her Connie, and I'm Frank.'

Frank has turned from the sink, is drying his hands with a checked teatowel. His hair is still thick, though almost completely white now, the moustache as bush-baby as ever. It gives him an air of eccentricity. The hawk eyes are still sharp: Martin remembers them from the day he first met Finnigan.

'Come down to the study and we'll talk things over. Thanks, Con.'

He leads the way down the carpeted hall to a small spiralling staircase at the end. Frank Finnigan's writing study. Martin imagines some venerable society deep underground, The Followers of Finnigan, people with funny hats reciting from *The Game of the Few*. But it's a fairly ordinary room, a reasonable size, messy, more bookshelves overflowing. Curtains are pulled across the french doors into the garden, but you can smell the sea out there. The only unusual feature is the large leather chair, a throne, squatting behind the desk. Frank takes his seat, and dominates the room like royalty. The oak desktop is large but more than half covered: computer, printer, fax, thesaurus, *Shorter Oxford* dictionary, blue-bound copy of Hemingway's collected stories, vase of wilting sweet william, packet of chewing gum, stone paperweight, stapler, stamps, phone book, empty box of shortbread, a small mountain of files, parking tickets, something scribbled.

'This has been my office for ten years – much bigger than my other ones. It's very useful having money, you know, now that Connie's finally got the hang of spending it.'

He's leaning back, hands behind his head, surveying the bookshelves behind. His eyes drop down to Martin who is poised on the edge of a hard chair facing the desk, and he suddenly swivels forward, leans his elbows on the desk, strokes his feathery upper lip.

'So, tell me, why do you want to do my biography?'

'I – I thought this was your idea.'

Schoolboy nerves, damn it.

'I guess you could say that.' Frank laughs, a gaudy guffaw, and fills his pipe with tobacco. 'I'm coming up to seventy, you know. Early next year. I get the feeling there aren't many more books in me.'

He glances up at Martin, as if to check his reaction, continues patting down tobacco. 'Never talked much to the press. Hardly done any interviews, not since '72 when there was all that palaver over *The Game of the Few*. I still go over to the States to do a reading now and again, just to remind the bastards I'm still alive, but apart from that I keep to myself.'

He strikes a match, sucks on the pipe as he lights it. A tiny fog of smoke obscures his face, his moustache flittering behind like a giant moth.

'They always get it wrong anyway, whether you talk to them or not. I've read so many fruitcake theories about my writing, none of those buggers know what they're talking about. Academics are the worst.' He looks up at Martin. 'Pack of ning-nongs.'

'So why ask me?'

Frank sucks on his pipe again, peers over his glasses until Martin is shrinking, feet barely touching the floor.

'Some nitwit in Hamilton wrote to me last year, asking to do my biography. You're not the only one to think of it you know.'

He sniffs. 'I wrote back, gave him much the same answer I gave you a few years earlier, and he rings up, says he's going to do it anyway. Malicious little prick, apparently he's been tracking down old friends already. Former friends. Beyond the bloody pale.'

'What's he got?'

'I don't know what he's got, that's the bloody trouble.'

'So, you're looking for a sanitised version instead?'

'Not sanitised, authorised. I'm not asking for a hagiography. I just want someone to do it right. If someone's going to be spinning myths about me, I'd rather it was a myth of my own choosing. I can get you a publisher all right, there's no worries about that.'

He gives a smug moustache twitch. It pricks Martin between the shoulders.

'I'm not into fantasy actually,' says Martin. 'If I do this, and I say if, I will want the truth, the whole truth and nothing but the truth.'

The smile vanishes, and Frank creaks backwards in his leather throne.

'Just joking, boy. Of course, of course. You'll have complete access to everything – all my manuscripts, letters, diaries. You can talk to whoever you want, I promise you. I'm just asking for the right to correct anything that's wrong, that's all. This bugger in Hamilton has some crackpot theory that he's trying to shape the material around. I just want someone to go into it open minded, no agendas.'

'Why me?'

Frank looks serious, teeth clicking on his pipe.

'I don't know, I like you. You remind me of me at your age.'

A cloud of smoke rises between them.

'You know that thesis you did when you were a student?'

'That was thirteen years ago. And I never sent it to you.'

'Somebody else did. Load of bollocks, of course.' Finnigan grins. 'But not complete bollocks. There was a section in there I rather liked, where you talked about childhood in New Zealand, how the children in my books tapped into a collective memory. Perceptive. I rather liked it.'

'My ideas have completely shifted since I did that thesis.'

'So they should have, I'd be worried if they hadn't. I know they have, anyway. I have to admit I've been spying on you.'

'What?'

'Your lectures. I've been sneaking into your NZ Lit lectures twice a week, sitting up the back.'

'Do you know how much people have to pay for those courses nowadays?'

Frank laughs. 'I thought, as a "cultural icon", I might be entitled to keep an ear on what's being said about me.'

'I suppose I have to concede that. But I won't necessarily agree that you know more about it.'

Martin realises he sounds like his own father.

Frank laughs, slaps his hand down abruptly on the desk.

'You're it, my boy. You are it. You're going to write my biography. What do you say?'

Martin takes a deep gulp of pipe smoke, a deep breath of Frank.

'I'm it.'

Frank claps his hand on the desk again.

'Excellent! You will be my Boswell, boy.'

Martin's always thought Boswell an arrogant, posturing fool.

The two men stand, shake hands on the deal, grin at each other in delight.

Wellington, 1982
Martin just has time between lectures to nip down to Cuba Street and go through the last second-hand bookshop on his list. He's been to five already and none have what he's looking for: Frank Finnigan's very first novel, *The Story of the River Stones*. Published in 1960, it's been out of print for twenty years. It's the last book he needs to complete his Finnigan set. He hums as he walks, hurrying to beat the threatened rain.

A rusty bell sounds dully as Martin opens the door to the shop. The man at the counter looks up from the book he's reading, then turns back to his pages like an old turtle momentarily disturbed from feeding. There's only one other person in the shop, a young woman browsing through the New Zealand shelves. Martin scans titles in the history section, waiting for her to move on, but can't contain himself for long and goes up behind her. She's wearing a long green coat with thick black stockings and old-fashioned shoes. He can't see the Fs for her coat, but checks out the rest of the alphabet. All the usual ones are there: a collection of Burnell he wouldn't mind, and a rare copy of an old Paul Rogers classic. Martin reaches out for it at the same time as the woman and their hands brush as they both pull back in embarrassment.

'Sorry.'

She has green eyes. Martin can't stop looking at them.

She looks away and he hurries to pull the book from the shelf, holds it out to her.

'You have it, I've read it already.'

'No, no, I was just looking.'

'Really. I'm looking for something else anyway.' He pushes it forward, until it's nearly touching her coat. He can smell gardenia. She accepts the book, thanking him shyly, and stands there, leafing through it.

'It's great. I strongly recommend it.'

He feels stupid, until she looks up again and the green of her eyes deflects him.

'What are you looking for?' she asks.

'A Frank Finnigan book, *The Story of the River Stones*. Do you know it?'

She shakes her thick black hair and smiles.

'You haven't read Finnigan? Not even *The Game of the Few*? But you must. It's brilliant. There must be a copy here . . . here you go. Take this one. God. *The Story of the River Stones!* Fantastic, I'd just about given up on finding a copy.'

He takes it from the shelf and looks through it: $25 for a tattered old hardback with coffee stains and some pages missing. Martin looks at the young woman and beams, then remembers the other book and thrusts it at her:

'You must read this one.'

She laughs. 'You're very enthusiastic. But I think I'll just take one today, thanks.'

She goes up to the counter and Martin trails behind her sadly. The shop assistant states the price and shoves the woman's book in a paper bag. She rifles through her purse and counts the cash into his palm as Martin fidgets behind her. He wishes she'd take the Finnigan book.

'Look, can I buy this one for you?'

She turns and frowns at him, a tiny crinkle in her forehead.

'No thank you.'

'It's just that it's such a great book . . . I'm not really a lunatic.' It comes out in a rush, and he colours.

The crinkle softens and she laughs again.

'Can I at least buy you a coffee?'

She hesitates. 'All right then.'

Triumphant, Martin puts the two books down on the counter and hands the shop assistant $40.

'My name's Martin, by the way.'

'I'm Alice.'

They walk down Cuba Street to a small cafe next to the fruit and vegetable shop. It's starting to spit. Alice orders a peppermint tea and goes to sit by the window while Martin takes his time paying and getting teaspoons. He puts the cups on the table and sits down next to her, nervous.

'So why do you like Frank Finnigan so much?'

'I've always liked him, his words, his sense of humour, I really like his sense of humour. People dismiss his stuff just because it's popular, but they're not reading him properly, he can be quite subtle, there are lots of different layers going on.'

The deluge of words surprises him. He doesn't normally talk this openly to people, not to women anyway. But he's confident on the subject, it's one of the few he has strong opinions about, and he's encouraged by Alice's interest.

'But I shouldn't rabbit on. You can tell I'm an English major. So what are you studying? Are you a student?'

'Well yes, but not at university. I'm studying nursing down in Canterbury.'

'Christchurch. So why are you in Wellington?'

'I'm just visiting my parents. They live at Eastbourne. My Mum's a nurse too.'

'Is that why you wanted to be one?'

'Don't know.' Her eyes flicker and she bends down and pulls up a stocking absently. 'I guess, but I kind of just like the idea of looking after people. What do you want to do for a job?'

'I'm not sure, maybe journalism, maybe become an academic.'

She wrinkles her nose slightly. He likes her, he likes her a lot.

Then she stands up and hoists her bag on her shoulder. 'Well, I better get going, I've got a hair appointment. Thanks for the coffee, and the reading advice. Maybe I'll see you round some time.'

Martin watches her with a feeling of slight panic.

'Here. Please.'

He hands her *The Game of the Few*. She takes it with a small smile and he watches her leave, the sheen of her dark hair glinting as she steps out into a sudden ray of sun, as if the clouds parted just for her. She disappears from view.

Martin checks his watch. He's missed his lecture but can still make the NZ Lit tutorial if he hurries. He leaves the cafe and winds his way through town, not looking at anyone. He walks quickly up Kelburn Parade and thinks of Alice.

The tutor, Janet Elderberry, taps her finger on the desk as he comes in.

'You're late.'

'Sorry.'

They're reading Eliza Hannay. Bugger. He sits in a corner chair and diligently heads up a page, doodles, looks out at the weak blue sky, the last of the rain clouds scudding away to the south.

'She was also a prolific journalist, and travelled as far as China at a time when few women did either thing. I've copied a few pieces of her reporting for you to read, and I highly recommend you read the first two books at least.'

Martin takes the pile of handouts from his neighbour, selects one and hands them on to the yawning girl on his right.

'Although the job of a journalist is compatible in many ways with that of a writer, you don't find many reporters making the transition.'

A niggling. Martin wakes up.

'What about Frank Finnigan?'

'What about him?'

'He was a journalist for years.'

'I'd never have guessed. And while we're on that topic, Martin, I'd like to see you after class about your last essay.'

So Finnigan wasn't on the list. So what? She should be glad of some original thinking. That's not how you get on, though, is it?

Martin knew she wouldn't like it. He keeps his head down for the rest of the class, fertilising the seed of his idea. By the end of the tutorial it's germinated tiny radicles which seize his brain, determined to cling to life. When the last of his fellow students has clomped out, Elderberry comes up and stands before his chair, hands him the essay.

'C.'

'It would have been higher but I had to penalise you for not writing on one of the designated options, Martin.'

Here we go.

'You're talented, intelligent. You'd go a lot further if you played by the rules.'

'I'm going to do my thesis on him.'

'Finnigan?' She laughs. 'Not if the English Department has anything to do with it, you're not.'

'What about freedom of speech? He's New Zealand's best-selling author, overseas anyway. Besides, I've already written to him and arranged an interview.'

A fib. He'd written, but Finnigan wrote back refusing: Read the books. And send it to me when you're finished, I could do with a good laugh.

'You won't find many secondary sources.'

'Won't take as long then, will it?'

Elderberry sighs. 'Let's discuss this later, I've got a lecture to get to.'

So has he, but instead he goes back to his flat. He lies on the ratty old couch in the late sun and watches particles of dust turn in the light. He thinks of Alice. There's something about her that scares him a little. The way she stood there in the bookshop with her feet apart, hands on her jutting-out hip bones, her chin set at that stubborn angle, eyes glimmering green. Perhaps she can see who he is.

Wellington, 1983
The thesis is driving Martin mad. He sits down at the electric typewriter again and stares at the blank paper. The problem is the structure: it's not working. He reads over the last page and tears it up. No secondary sources is a problem, actually. He goes to the library and flicks through books on similar subjects, slumps in a chair and closes his eyes, thinking. It's no good. He goes home and spends the rest of the afternoon reading *Plums*, Finnigan's collection of short stories.

That night Martin decides he's better off forgetting about the stories and leaving the poetry out altogether. He'll tell his supervisor he'll focus just on the six novels, one section per novel, that's much more manageable. He goes to bed and sleeps well for the first time in months.

The next morning he's in the university bookshop, picking out a birthday present for his mother, when he stops dead in front of the new-releases table. A small sign sits atop piles of freshly minted editions, still smelling of ink: **Frank Finnigan's latest!** *The Bones of My Father*. **Only $24.95**.

Fuck.

He needs Alice. He catches a stand-by flight to Christchurch late that morning.

She frowns when she opens the door and sees him there, looking sheepish. She's just about to finish her exams; sits her final one the next day. He's forgotten. He tries to make up for it, acts bashful, puppyish: she used to like it when he was pathetic. Now she just gets that stubborn look in her eye, her jaw sets at that angle. He's about to get angry with her – he's come all this way, can't she see he needs her now – when she relents.

'All right, you can stay. But you go out all afternoon and don't come back until dinner, and you sleep on the couch tonight. After the exam you can have all my attention.'

Martin does as she asks, and wanders around Christchurch for the rest of the afternoon. Ducklings are out in force along the Avon, paddling happily. They make him more depressed. He goes back to the flat about six, bringing bread as a peace offering, and finds Alice more welcoming, although she's still firm about the couch: he will 'disturb her focus'. Nonetheless, he creeps into her room that night. She's sleeping, her skin pale and gently freckled, like a smooth white beach, the odd dark shell nestled. He touches his lips to her face. So smooth and so warm. He tiptoes back to the couch.

The next day he waits for her outside the exam room.

'How was it?'

'It doesn't matter, it's over!'

They kiss, and smile, and kiss again.

'Did you put that bag in the car?'

'Yeah. What's it for?'

'We might need it where we're going.'

And she drags him by the hand to the parked car, demands the keys, and jumps in the driver's seat:

'Let's go.'

He slips his seatbelt on discreetly as Alice reverses. She's a terrible driver.

'Where are we going exactly?'

'You'll see.'

He's beginning to worry by the time they get to Darfield and are still heading towards the mountains.

'We're not going skiing, are we?'

'There's no snow, idiot. It's November.'

They reach Bealey, just before Arthur's Pass, and Alice turns up a dirt road to a group of scattered houses.

'I've borrowed a friend's bach. Isn't it fabulous?'

Martin wishes he'd known where they were going. He might not feel so unsettled. He gets out of the car and follows Alice into the little wooden house. A tiny kitchen, lounge with wood fire, old sofas covered in multi-coloured cushions, board games stacked on a small coffee table, and up the rickety stairs two small bedrooms.

'Where's the loo?'

'Ah, that's the interesting bit.'

She shows him outside. It's a long-drop.

Martin shudders.

'Is there a shower?'

'Yup.'

With a flourish Alice pulls across an old curtain to reveal a showerhead on a handle, and a bright yellow bucket.

'Great.'

'Oh, come on. It'll be fun. There's no electricity, but that makes it lovely and cosy at night.'

'No electricity?'

He notices all the candle stubs weeping skirts of wax and looks around gloomily as Alice brings the bags in. It seems like the first time there's been just the two of them. He wonders if she's nervous. If he is.

Later they walk down to the river. It's warm, although the trees are still coated in the fresh green of spring. Alice leaps across the river boulders and Martin watches, notices how much easier it is for him to breathe here. He leaps after her. They sit on the bank, see who can skip stones the furthest, and she asks,

'Do you love me, Martin?'

His reply comes automatically, without thinking.

'Of course.'

Only after he speaks does he consider the question. He sits quietly, skips a large flat stone clear across the water – six, seven skips. He smiles, sees Alice looking at him.

'Why?'

This time he does consider it. Because you love me.

'Because you're beautiful and kind and wonderful to be with, and . . . and you understand me.'

She laughs. Her throat is long and white, like a bird's.

'Well you're right on the first three anyway!'

And she jumps up and runs along the riverbank, her white skirt flapping, a heron.

'Come on.'

Martin runs after her and she laughs a little and they run faster. He catches her just as she reaches a group of trees and swings around a trunk, breathless. They fall to the ground, laughing, and he tickles her, kisses her, slips his hand up her skirt, along her legs, and slides a finger into her pants, making her gasp, an involuntary little expulsion of air that he opens his mouth for and swallows. She pulls him closer and he can hear blood beating at his temples; feels his cock hardening beneath her hand fumbling at his zip. Their clothes are awkwardly shoved aside, her brown knees spread wide, and he's inside her, a strange silence broken only by the click of her hip bone and the rasp of their breath.

Afterwards they lie side by side on their backs, looking up at the sky through a criss-crossing green canopy of tree branches. He loves the pinkness of her lips, the softness of her eyelashes. The curves of their bodies fit together like segments of fruit. Martin thinks of their earlier conversation.

'Do you love me?'

She rolls towards him and traces the outline of his lips with a long piece of grass.

'So much it scares me.'

Her voice is low, and he watches her black pupils widen, spill over to swamp the green of her irises.

She loves him.

Something floods his head and enters his blood, slowly

travels through his body, tingling.

'Will you marry me?'

'Yes.'

They embrace, clinging, unable to look in each other's faces, and he wonders what they have just done.

Christchurch, 1985

Martin examines the small room. Desk there, facing the window, so he can see the green lawn and trees – no, maybe facing the wall so he won't get distracted. Filing cabinet and shelves there; under the desk that ugly rug Alice gave him; all those inbuilt bookshelves on the side: fantastic. He counts the boxes. Nine. Just as well there's all those bookshelves. He slices down the stomach of a box with a scalpel and the musty smell of ink on mildewed paper rises. He bends to inhale and Alice, passing the door, laughs at him.

'Get on with it.'

It's good to have his own study for once, especially now he's tutoring part-time. It won't be long till he's full-time. Martin works slowly, handling each volume as if the pages could crumble to dust, and stacking the books carefully in alphabetical categories for later shelving: English lit, history, pol sci, perhaps a separate New Zealand section; then divisions of British, American, anthologies. Definitely a separate poetry section. He sorts each stack, splits them into smaller piles, making sure they're still alphabetical. Here's the framed photo of his Masters graduation: why had he ever thought a moustache suited him? He puts it on the desk and looks back at the books. He needs a system. Martin examines the labels on the boxes until he finds the one he's looking for.

When Alice passes the door again, he's sitting wedged between boxes in a corner of the room, his long legs folded up under him like some sort of insect, inscribing titles on tiny cards.

'I'm devising a card catalogue system.'

'They're not matchbox cars, Martin.'

He'd spent hours as a child sorting cars into categories: colour, make, year, number plates. Order. Something to hold on to. He prints carefully on another card: *Winter, Jack. Collected Poems. Oxford University Press, 1979.* File, poetry section. Perhaps a separate New Zealand poetry section. He feels inordinately pleased.

The next box is full of thesis material. He should throw it out really, but flips through his lit crit papers and uncovers a copy of the thesis itself, hiding. Only just passed in the end, after three rewrites. Stuffy bastards never got over the subject matter. So much for being original: no one approves.

He opens to the introduction.

Frank Finnigan's The Game of the Few has sold more copies overseas than any other New Zealand book. An almost instant blockbuster in the United States when it was published in 1972, Finnigan's fourth novel rode a wave of the public imagination in such a way that the book's themes became synonymous with the themes of the time. The title itself passed into common everyday usage, transformed into what could now be considered a cliché.

He flips forward a few pages. This attitude towards interpretative solipsism, he's still not sure about it.

Thus we examine the claim that a text can mean anything a reader chooses. We remove the Author and it becomes clear that it is futile to claim to decipher the text. Once a text is awarded an Author, it is, thereby, limited. However, by refusing to assign an ultimate meaning to a text, we are liberated. Such an activity is revolutionary, as the refusal to fix such a meaning is, in the end, the refusal of God himself.

He had thought to impress his superviser. But he's undermined his own argument with those assessments of texts as New Zealand works, those passing notes of biographical, historical detail. And that was his favourite section. The lack of consistency blows apart the initial assertion: perhaps there's a sub-conscious yearning for reason there. No longer a church-going subscriber, Martin secretly believes in God.

Why, then, has he succumbed to academia? Again this unexpected sense of despair. His legs ache with it; he stretches them out. He must develop his own ideology here at Canterbury, not simply squeeze into uncomfortable accommodations – structuralist, post-structuralist, deconstructionist theory. It may be convenient, but it's simply ridiculous to kill off the author in such a way. Perhaps that's why he never sent a copy to Finnigan.

Alice is calling him for lunch.

'Why the glum-bum? Cataloguing not as much fun as you thought?'

She gives him a quick hug, but Martin turns her back around to him, holds her longer. He smiles at her weakly.

'I just found my thesis. What a load of crap.'

He sits down at the table as Alice dishes out steaming bowls of soup, the spiralling smell of lemongrass. She's laughing.

'Less than a year ago you thought that load of crap was brilliant.'

'I confused "brilliant" with "finished".'

He presses too hard buttering, and the bread rips to expose the gleaming white eye of the plate beneath.

'Well at least now you're a tutor you'll be able to spot crap.'

Martin looks at her bleakly.

'Sorry,' she says.

They sip soup. He likes the noise she makes when she eats.

'Why do you think it's crap, hon?'

'All that abolished author thing. It's just melodrama. If we destroy the author, on what basis do we evaluate his work? I was just being lazy, lazy in accepting others' doctrines, lazy in not uncovering my own.'

'Do you think you've discovered your own now?'

'Yeah. Maybe. I don't know. If I was doing it again I'd throw all that deconstructionist garbage out the window, find out what Finnigan thought he was saying. Maybe that's the true meaning, not just what any old ignorant reader thinks.'

'But how do you find out the author's meaning?'

'Why not ask him?'

'But what if he's dead?'

'Finnigan's not dead.'

'He might not be, but plenty of authors are.'

'I don't know. You look for clues, I guess. You search their lives, their other works. Unveil the patterns of their minds.'

'Sounds difficult.'

Martin stares into his bowl of soup and watches the noodles slowly swirling to form a language, an idea.

'Where are you going?'

'Thanks for lunch.'

'What are you doing?'

'I'm going to write to Finnigan, asking to be his biographer.'

Wellington, May 1996

Martin waits for the cable car to slide steadily down into place, clang-clanging its bell. He's tired, and something is pounding his temples. Instead of the usual weekday mass of scruffy students disembarking there's a handful of weekend tourists and a few mums with pushchairs. Martin smiles at one, feels a pang of guilt. He should've taken Lance to soccer this morning, instead of wasting his Saturday morning at that damn conference. It hadn't even been any use: the keynote speaker he'd gone to hear was replaced at the last minute with that twit from Auckland, and Elderberry wasn't even there to approve his presence. That disappointed frown on Lance's face this morning, mirrored by Alice standing behind.

The boy's growing up fast. Next weekend there'll be more time.

The cable car doors glide open with a faint snake hiss and Martin steps on, chooses a seat down the back. Only four other people get on, a couple with a young child and an older man who sits in front of him. He checks his watch: just after 12. Still time before the second innings to take Alice and Lance out for ice cream to redeem himself for this morning. The car reaches its first stop, opens and closes its doors for no one. Sun glints on the tracks behind as Martin looks back into the black mouth of the tunnel.

That bloody dinner they have to go to tonight. At least Roger and Jane will be there, otherwise Alice could well have bailed. She doesn't like the rest of the faculty; he doesn't much either actually. Peter Cray, for instance: he's been going on recently about Martin's upcoming sabbatical, how he should get on to some serious research, prove himself. But none of the suggested topics appeal, not remotely. He should've stayed at Canterbury: there was none of this pressure.

He stands to get off and nearly bumps into the older man who is rising from his seat. Martin apologises, and gives way to the man, who grumbles under his stiff white hank of a moustache as he pushes past. Martin feels as if he's forgotten something. He shakes his head a little as he gets out, and looks across the sparkling harbour. Stuff the department: nowhere can beat Wellington on a fine day. He walks down the road in the sun, whistling.

'I'm home!'

There's no reply, so he calls again, less cheerfully. The

cricketers are still out at lunch. Damn. He flings his keys on the kitchen bench.

Martin starts to make himself a sandwich and notices the morning's mail lying unopened next to the phone. Bills; postcard from friends of Alice – lucky buggers sunning and surfing in Bali; and a letter addressed to him, in writing he doesn't recognise. He turns it over and reads the scrawled sender's name: F. Finnigan. Good God. The man on the cable car. He opens the envelope.

There's just one piece of paper, a few lines sprawled in a spider of black ink.

Dear Martin Wrightson,

I found a letter from you dated 1985 – I never throw anything out you'll be pleased to hear. I seem to remember I was rather rude. I've changed my mind. Call me.

Frank

Martin is sitting at the kitchen table, letter still in hand, when Alice and Lance come in.

'Who's died?' she asks.

Wellington, July 1996
Martin calls out as soon as he gets in the door.

'I'm going to do it!'

'Hang on, I'm coming.'

He hears some thumping upstairs before Alice appears, dishevelled and flushed.

'That bloody shelf's come down again. I told you it would.'

'I'm going to do it, Alice. I'm going to do it.'

'The shelf?'

'The biography.'

'Are you sure? What's he like?'

Martin takes off his jacket, goes to put his bag in the study. Alice follows.

'Tell me what happened.'

'Well, he just asked me to do it and I said yes. I worked it out on the way home, I'll start it during my sabbatical.'

'I thought we were going to the States.'

'That was just one idea, Ali. This way we stay settled in Wellington. You get to keep your job, Lance stays at the same school, it'll be much better.'

'Are you sure this is what you want? Biographies take years. You won't get it done in time.'

'Doesn't matter, I'll do it part-time after the sabbatical. He's great, Ali. He was a journalist, he's been to war, lived in Asia, there's plenty of meat in it. Now I know what I'm doing, and I'll be able to compare the works to the life, discover the author's meaning, the real meaning. The truth.'

He hugs her, lifting her off the ground.

'Put me down, idiot.'

'Aren't you excited?'

He puts her down, searches her sea-dark eyes for emotion. Please.

She smiles, pats his cheek a little. 'I'm glad you're excited, hon. I haven't seen you like this in a long time.'

'I still get this excited about you, lady.'

He picks her up again, whirls her round the room until they collapse on the couch. This is what it used to be.

'So, what's he like?'

'Frank? Quite old, about seventy, very down to earth, very Kiwi really. Funny guy. Gruff but charming.'

The booming laugh, firm handshake, blue hawk eyes under sprouting brows: vulnerability under camouflage. He likes him.

'You know Rex Widdens in *The Game of the Few*? He's kind of like him.'

'Uh oh. I never liked him. Too self-absorbed, insecure. Is Finnigan insecure?'

'I don't think so, no. He's very confident, very comfortable in himself. He knows what he's doing, and if no one else likes it, to hell with them, that sort of thing.'

'Is he married?'

'Yes, I met his wife, Connie. She's very quiet, writes poetry I think. You'll have to meet them. I'm sure I'll be practically living round there by the end of it.'

She pummels his chest. 'As long as you remember you're married to me.'

'I know you're sick of me working so hard, but I'll have to put a lot into this.'

'That's okay, as long as you promise to enjoy yourself. It's when you're working hard and are miserable that I feel it.'

Her eyes are hard green stones, flickering through river water.

'I promise I'll enjoy this.'

'Good. Maybe it'll make you start wanting to write fiction again yourself.'

'No.'

He pushes her off and goes to the bookshelves. There's so much to do.

'Guess I better read all these again. Nine novels, two collections of short stories. There must be more analytical criticism of him by now. We're not very well off for biographies. I'll have to go the library and stock up.'

So much to do. That's what's been missing.

Lance is calling out from the other room – he's made something new – and Alice goes to give her approval. Martin picks up one of the biographies and opens to the introduction.

'The biographer's role is to reproduce the truth as closely as is humanly possible. Henry James once described it as a quest of imaginative experience which could be one of the greatest observed adventures of mankind.'

So. Let the quest begin.

Chapter 2

'Funny, the things one remembers.'

'Where do we begin?'

'I suppose at the beginning.'

Martin shuffles his chair closer to the desk; the morning sun spilling in the french doors is making it difficult for him to see Frank.

'Do you think we could close the curtains?'

'What for? It's a beautiful morning.'

Martin doesn't push it. Now, to begin. He checks the tape recorder again – red light on, tiny wheels spinning; looks at his list of questions.

'Why don't we start with your family, your childhood.'

'I was born in Nelson, on January 6, 1927. No, let's start before that, with my grandfather, Jacob Finnigan, Irish of course. He arrived in 1861 on the brig the *Seagull* when he was fourteen years old. The ship landed where Lambton Quay is now; I can remember him pointing it out to me once. He told me a grand story about the sailing across from England – he was quite a storyteller, the Dad. That's what the family called him, my father and all my aunts and uncles, the Dad.'

Frank leans back in the brown leather arms of his chair, strokes the swelling of whiskers on his lip. This is not what Martin wants exactly, but maybe it's better not to interrupt. Frank's pose is fit for oratory.

'The Dad said he'd never seen such beautiful hills as the

Wellington hills ringing the harbour. I guess you'd be pleased to see anywhere after spending six months on a bloody boat. Horses brought them up from the beach, he told me, a dray drawn by horses. He stayed in Wellington for the first year.'

What does it feel like, stroking it like that, soft and feathery like bird breast, or coarse like brush bristles? Maybe – no, Alice would hate it.

'In 1862 he went to Nelson to join his older brother James as a storekeeper, and eventually ended up taking over the business after James got ill. He was a very hard-working man, Jacob. Honest labour is the secret of success: that was his motto. He drummed that into his kids. He died when I was young but I have very vivid memories of him, of both my grandparents. They were what you might call forceful personalities. We often spent holidays round their place. The Dad taught me to play euchre, and he would *slap* the joker down on the table. It used to give me quite a fright. I was only a little blighter.'

The bellow of laughter makes Martin jump, echoing the ghost of the child. He can imagine Frank doing the same thing to his own grandchildren.

'And your grandmother?'

'Nellie. She was very much a woman of her time. She served in my grandfather's shop after James got ill. That's how they met. I guess the Dad was about twenty-five, Nan fifteen. They didn't think so much of age differences then. She was a very religious woman; she used to read the scriptures to me. It didn't do me any harm, but it didn't do me much good either. We used to wag Sunday school, my brother and me, and go boating on the lake. I remember the bloody hard seats at church. She would give us a penny to take to Sunday school – a penny was a coin of some importance in those days – but we'd spend it on lollies. You could buy a great lump of chocolate for a penny.'

The sun glints on the edge of the computer, dives into the black of the screen, suffuses to a dark chocolate melt. Martin's thoughts merge with it: grandparents, parents, what do they tell of Frank? He tries to imagine this whiskery old fellow as a little boy, hands sticky with chocolate, grubby knees and a cheeky smile. He would have been cheeky all right.

'They both lived to a great old age, especially the Dad: he was eighty-six. Good genes there. I remember his funeral quite clearly. I would have been – what, six, seven. It was at a wee church in Waimea West, and the service seemed to go on forever. I was getting quite antsy, being so young. When we finally got out of the church, I followed the pallbearers over to the grave and said loudly, "That's a bloody great hole!" Boy, did I get a hiding. Nan called me "a holy terror".'

That dawn-breaking rooster cackle again.

Martin smiles insipidly. He's not at all in control, and he knows it. It feels as if he's being given a lecture in his father's study.

'My older cousins were very impressed. There were tons of cousins always around – all those aunts and uncles, you see. We used to run in packs, terrorise the adults. There was this girl called Leah, Zeenie's daughter. We went to Nelson Central School together, were in the same class. But she got rheumatic fever when she was young and was a sickly thing. Zeenie used to say she "suffered from nerves". I probably didn't help. I used to play all sorts of tricks on her. She'd believe anything.

'I remember once I convinced her a bee had flown down her throat when she was asleep. She made me look and I told her I could see its wings. She went mad, even believed she could hear it buzzing. I took her down to the chemist, Mr. . . what the hell was it . . . Hinchcliff, and she asked him to look down to see if he could see the bee. He was very amused and said no, he couldn't see it but he'd have a close look after serving the other customers. We waited and waited: I'm sure he was telling the other customers, because now and then one would look over at us and smile. Leah was sitting there all eyes, convinced she could feel the bee in her throat and gulping a lot. Finally Hinchcliff had another look and said he was fairly sure a bee had not flown down there. I had a terrible time trying to persuade her not to tell her mother. I was in enough trouble for telling whoppers already. Leah's dead now, died last year.'

Frank pauses and looks out the window to the garden. Martin shifts in his chair. This is not really what he's looking for. There are too many incidentals, all jumbled. If he just gets the history now he can sort out what anecdotes he wants to use later. He feels inadequate, a fraud, is angry at the feeling. What is he looking for?

'Perhaps you could give me a few more details – dates, full names, that sort of thing.'

Frank's eyes snap. 'They're all dead now, what does it matter? You're meant to be asking about me, not them.'

'Yes, I know, but it might be useful. You have to let me do this my way, Frank.'

The white eyebrows bristle, slowly subside, two wiry cats stretching, settling down to sleep.

'Those publishers I mentioned, by the way. They said they'd be interested in seeing the first draft. I'll give you the number.'

'I'm sure I could find my own publisher if necessary.'

'Yes, yes, but let's face it, you don't know much about all this business, do you?'

'Do you want me to do this or not?'

'All right, keep your hair on. What do you want to know?'

That's it, take control. What *does* he want to know?

'Let's start with your parents, your aunts and uncles, a list of their names, when and where they were born.'

'Jesus, I don't know all that. I bet you don't know your own family. Some of them were dead before I was born.'

Martin tries to look severe.

'All right, let me think. The eldest was Ernest. He must have been born the year after they were married, so about 1874. There was Gwendoline, and Eveline, a few years later. I remember

Zeenie, she was just before my Dad, William. He was the youngest of the nine, born in 1890. The others . . . I remember there was an Uncle Eliot and Uncle . . . Clarry, he was killed in the Great War. How many's that? There must have been a couple more girls – oh, Olive and . . . Libby, or Elizabeth. That's it.'

He's very pleased with himself for remembering, and Martin is pleased with getting it out of him, but it's just a list of names. Is this what he will end up with? Dry names and numbers, the odd anecdote. He blinks uncertainly, checks the tape is still spinning.

'My brother Tom did a family tree a few years ago. I'll get that for you, shall I?'

'That would be great.'

Martin looks down at his carefully ordered questions.

'How about some photos? We're bound to have stacks of photos. Connie! I'll go see where Connie's put them. Hang on.'

Frank creaks up the stairs, leaving Martin sitting forlornly like a lifeboat bobbing on an ocean, out of his depth. How do biographers do it? How does a grandfather, grandmother, five aunts and three uncles, a mother and father, a brother called Tom, how does this add up to Frank? Where are the keys to it? Martin abandons ship, stands up and stretches, wanders over to the bookshelf behind the desk. Here are the books, some of them written in this very place, this desk. What a mess. He picks up the Hemingway and feels the weight, spots a scrap of paper slid partly under the ink blotter, and tugs it free. The hand is spider-scrawled, large loops of blue ink:

Grandfather, Grandmother
Funeral
Leah and the bee
Schooldays, Mr Thornton
Swimming Baths
Dad

So, it's all a show. He's going to say exactly what he wants to say and nothing more. Manufactured emotion. So much for the truth. Martin's shoulders itch in anger and he can feel his ears filling with blood. He's being taken for some 'authorised' fool – well, wait and see.

Frank is approaching the stairs as Martin puts back the paper and goes to stand by the french doors, looking out into a mass of dappled colour in the garden.

'I found some of the early ones.'

Two large photo albums are cradled in Frank's arms. He slaps them on the desk, and a couple of tiny black and white prints go fluttering to the floor like lost souls. Martin stoops to the rescue.

'Who's this?'

'Oh, I don't know. Here, take a look at these ones.'

Martin goes round to Frank's side of the desk, holding out one corner of a picture, a little girl in ringlets and tutu, a toe pointed severely.

'Who's this, Frank?'

Frank glances at the photo, then at Martin.

'I think that's my mother. But here, look, here are my grandparents.'

He points to another faded black and white. A large bearded man sits in the foreground, concentrating on the camera as if it were a problem to be solved. Behind stands a tall woman in a long silk dress with a bustle, white lace at the neck, surrendering. She smiles sadly at Martin.

'And this one, this one shows all the kids.'

Martin gently lowers Frank's hand, not looking at the picture.

'What are you doing? I thought you wanted photos.'

'Sit down, Frank.'

'Why? I'll be buggered if you're going to order me around in my own home. There are plenty of . . .'

'Sit down, Frank.'

Frank sits, glares.

'Got the photos all picked out, have you Frank? Going to show me a couple of the old Dad, your aunts and uncles, maybe one of Leah gulping down the bee, were you?'

'What the hell. . .'

Martin bends over the chair, menacing almost.

'Then maybe you could go on to show me one of Mr Thornton, whoever he is, and one of the swimming baths. I'm sure there's a nice little anecdote to go along with that one, isn't there, Frank? Perhaps we could talk about your father then – only if you feel comfortable, of course.'

He moves Hemingway to the other side of the desk, exposing the scrap of paper. The glare is transferred to it, dissolves. Frank drops down into innocence.

'All right, so I'm caught. But you can't blame me for wanting a few props, a few reminders. My memory's not as good as it used to be.'

Martin brings his hard chair around to sit by Frank.

'Now we're going to do it my way.' He holds up the tutu girl again. 'Who's this, Frank?'

'I told you, my mother.'

'Tell me about her.'

Frank holds the print by its white corners, looks again at the tiny ballet dancer:

'Wasn't she beautiful?'

He clears his throat, glances at Martin, then concentrates on the photo.

'They told me she had long hair until just before I was born. Lovely long blonde hair. My father often used to urge her to grow it back, but she wouldn't. She'd only do as she wanted to do, my mother. I don't have many pictures of her as a child. I guess photographs were a luxury then, I don't know.'

He knocks his pipe on the side of an ashtray and gets out fresh tobacco.

'She died in childbirth, you know.'

'No, I didn't know. Was it Tom?'

'No, eight years after that, another boy. He died too.'

Keep going, keep it going. He'll close up in the face of sympathy.

'Tell me what you remember of her.'

Frank looks down at the photo in his left hand, puffs on his pipe.

'One of my earliest memories is of her singing to me at night. It must have been summer, because the window was open and I was watching the long white curtain flickering in the night breeze. I was fascinated by it, couldn't take my eyes off the thing, swooping in and out with the wind, like a dancer in a long white dress. My mother must have noticed me watching it; maybe she thought it frightened me, because she drew it back and went to close the window, but then she saw the sky and stopped. "Look, Frankie," she said, "look at the beautiful stars." Apparently that's when I said my first word, so my mother told me later.'

'Stars?'

'No. "Frankie". Although my mother said it came out "Fankee", as if I was thanking her.'

'Tell me more about her.'

Frank puts down the photo and puffs again. Martin breathes in the tobacco; he likes the smell, bitter-sweet, wonders how it tastes. Frank passes him another photo: his mother in her early twenties, a pretty fair-haired woman smiling at the camera, a hint of Frank around her brows, her eyes.

'My mother. My mother was a school teacher, at least she was before we were born, my brother Tom and I. As I said, I was born in 1927 and Tom followed two years later, May 1929. After we both went to school, she took up teaching again. Times were hard and, before he took over the bakery, my father couldn't get work, so she got a part-time job at Nelson Central School, until she fell pregnant again.'

Martin thinks how Alice will laugh at the phrase.

'She was a good teacher. Both Tom and I could read before we even started school. She loved books, I guess I got that from her. It certainly wasn't my father. What was she like? I guess I don't really know what she was like. She died when I was ten and my father never really talked about her afterwards. You didn't, in those days.'

He looks at Martin as if he doesn't expect him to understand, but he does. His family never talked about things either.

'Just tell me what you remember.'

'I remember her hands, she had long hands. I used to lie with my head in her lap, when I was very little, and stroke her fingernails with my thumb. She didn't like that, said it gave her the willies. Her hands weren't soft, don't think that. They were hardened by work and the sun, brown in summer with little dark freckles. They could give little boys a fair good whack too. We got plenty of spankings. Not like today, where you practically get locked up for raising your voice to a kid. Never did us any harm, the odd whacking – probably did us good. We would have been uncontrollable otherwise. That's the problem with kids today, no discipline, no respect for their elders.'

Martin thinks of Lance. He can't imagine spanking him.

'Did you respect your mother?'

'I certainly did! I wouldn't have been able to get away with not respecting her, or my father. And I demanded the same respect from my kids in turn. That's how it should be.'

'Let's go back to your mother. You haven't told me her name.'

'Deirdre, Deirdre Widdens.'

'Widdens?'

Martin regrets letting his surprise show. The tension between them vibrates like a silent string.

'Yes.'

Frank looks at Martin, face unreadable.

'She was born on April 1, 1900. Made it easy to remember her birthdays. There must be some other photos in here.' He flicks through one of the albums. 'There's the aunts, you see, that's Olive and Elizabeth. But you don't want to know about them, do you, boy?'

'Some other time perhaps.'

'Here we go, here's my parents' wedding. Mother looks like she's wearing that bedroom curtain.'

He cackles, relaxed at last.

'How old was she there?'

'Well, that was 1925, so twenty-five. Dad was ten years older. Still, he looks younger, don't you think?'

'He looks a bit like you.'

The same nose, the oddly feminine lips, the line of the mouth ready to tighten into a disapproving grimace or fall open into a guffaw.

'Like me? Do you think? I guess, maybe he does. Connie always said he did, but I could never see it. I think Ian looks more like him.'

'Ian?'

'My son. Here's a photo of him, looking like a bloody fairy.'

'I can see the resemblance, but also through you.'

The son, in a gaudy Hawaiian shirt, sports the beginnings of a moustache, a youthful version struggling to reach the same lushness of his father's upper lip.

'I don't look much like my mother anyway. Here's a photo of her with her hair cut short, and that's me, that little blighter dressed up like a girl. Don't know why they did that back then. Bloody humiliating. And there's Mum with Zeenie. Zeenie was the only one of Dad's sisters she liked. Maybe I picked that up from her. She liked The Dad and Nellie well enough, though. We often used to spend holidays with them.'

So, we're piecing together the family relationships, threading together a cat's cradle. Who else is there?

'What about your other grandparents, her parents?'

'I never met them, or at least if I did I can't remember it. I recall Mother going off for a week once, down to Dunedin, and I think that must have been for her father's funeral. I guess her mother had already died. Yes, she must have. I don't know anything about her. Quiet, I think, gentle. Don't know why I think that. Her father was a sea captain and boat builder. I remember her telling me stories about how he had sailed to Dunedin in one of his own boats, met her mother and fallen in love. My mother grew up there, near Anderson's Bay. She was always interested in boats, maybe they reminded her of her father. She would often take us boys down to watch the ships sail in Nelson Harbour. We'd walk around the port hills and choose a picnic spot with a view of the harbour entrance to see all the big Anchor Line and Union boats come in. The *Hawea*, the *Rotorua*, the *Takapuna*, the *Penguin*. That was Tom's favourite. We loved those picnics. I think Mum did too.'

Martin feels uncomfortable, wonders if this is how a priest feels hearing confession. It's not shocking stuff, but it seems odd to hear Frank express what comes close to emotion. He watches Frank shyly, but the man is taking no notice of him, leaning back in his chair, chewing on his pipe, his bristling white eyebrows bunched together in thought. A gentle puff of smoke rises.

'She was a very intelligent woman. She lived in the days when secondary education wasn't free and she was very proud of the fact that she'd won a scholarship to go to Otago Girls' High School. She used to talk a lot about that. It was the first girls' public school in the southern hemisphere, and the principal was very much a lady, prim and proper. Just as well Tom and I were boys. It's funny, you know. When I was in Dunedin a few years ago, there was a museum exhibition on the suffrage centennial and there were some school reports up on the wall, and there in faded ink was one of my mother's reports. She'd come second in Latin and got 97 percent in English. But what was a surprise to me was she was top in science, because she always said she didn't like that.'

'What did she like?'

'Well, she was always a keen reader. She made us join the public library, just because she liked going there, I think. We would get out all those detective stories and *Boy's Own* annuals and she would make us carry home a huge pile of books she'd chosen. She was mad on reading. She told great bed-time stories too. Just made up out of her own head, stories about monkeys. I haven't thought of those in years.'

There's no need for a list of questions. Just listen to the man.

'So it was her who encouraged you first to write?'

'I don't really know. I suppose it could have been. I used to write for the *Nelson Evening Mail*'s kids page, Dot's Little Folks. And I remember now there was some club at primary school where we wrote our own magazines. I would take them home and Dad would roar with laughter, but Mum would always say my stories were very good and slip me a sweet or a pastry.'

Another string threaded through the lattice.

'Did she write herself?'

'No, I don't think so. She certainly showed an interest in writing, but you see she had no outlet for it. That could well have been an unfulfilled ambition.'

Frank pauses, looks disarmed.

'I never realised that before.'

'Maybe we should leave it there for today.'

'Okay, boy, whatever you say. After all, we're doing it your way from now on, eh?'

Martin sits at his desk and feels empty. He fiddles with his pen, goes over his notes again. The computer screen shimmers, and he notices the diffused light has turned his fingertips green. He types the heading, TRANSCRIPT 1. He will have to prepare better questions next time. He is sure the key is in the questions: they determine the material, shape Frank's answers, what he says and how he says it. He must phrase them exactly, in order to provoke emotion or logic accordingly. The right doors will open if the right questions are asked.

Martin goes over his early notes, jumbled messily over A4 pages. He must get those in some sort of order, then he will know how to proceed. He just needs structure. Alice has given him a new card catalogue. It sits on the desk, still in its box, glistening. He thinks she bought it for him as a joke, and maybe he has shown too much pleasure in it. But it's just what he needs. He opens the box and gets out the cards, sealed in plastic like slices of processed cheese, and arranges them within the catalogue. At the end he's missing the letters from T to Z; he eventually discovers them on the back of numbers 4–10. Useless bloody thing.

Martin puts it to one side. This is just procrastination; he knows what he has to do. He must answer some basic questions before he begins. He cracks open the spine of a brand new exercise book. First page, Frank Finnigan, underline in red pen. Now the questions of presentation, structure, the perils of selection. He's still struggling with the chronology; it's going to be hard to avoid foreshadowing or flashbacks, but they could be useful. Should he stick to straight narrative, cradle to hypothetical grave, or go for the topical, splitting Frank into various parts? It might be easier to construct a portrait, using something essay-like – an informal, discursive style. Stracheyesque perhaps. But that tendency to create pastiche makes Martin uneasy.

Then there's the question of how to handle the works themselves. Do they dominate? He's coming round to the view that the critiques should not be separated out, but contained within the main text. The awareness of recurring themes, the symbolism of the works, can then be more clearly linked with the life. Here are the keys to the private mythology of the individual. He'll have to consider the justification of psychoanalysis. Martin notes down a series of questions and possible answers, quickly covering the first blank page with his precise handwriting, then the next, a black trail of ink to be followed. The more he writes, the more the concept clarifies in his mind until, after nine neat pages, it has crystallised into a brilliant trapezoid, as hard and clear as glass glinting in late afternoon sun.

He hears Alice open the study door, and quickly covers the card catalogue with a book.

'How's it going, hon?'

He is silent for a moment, thinking.

'Lytton's right. It's as difficult to write a good life as to live one.'

Alice laughs. 'Never mind, maestro. You'll be rewarded in the end. Want a cup of tea?'

'In a minute.'

He should make topic headings for the cards. They will point the direction. He needs a methodology to bring order, otherwise chaos will overwhelm. He lists subheadings on a fresh piece of paper: early childhood; school years; extended family (subcategories: grandparents, parents, brother, others); friends (subcategories according to time periods); journalism (*Nelson Evening Mail*, *Evening Post*, Hong Kong, NZPA, etc.); Connie; children (subcategories: Nancy, Ian); works (subcategories per text); criticism; awards. That will do for now, that's something to go on with. Two transcripts to type up: Frank and Sid Hewlitt. Sid won't take long. It was a lucky break, running into Sid yesterday. Frank so effusive: 'My best mate, mate. You've got to talk to him.' They hadn't seen each other for twenty years. So much for matey-mate. Still, probably one of the only friends from the school years, and he'd landed in his lap just like that. Sid went on and on about what a great writer Frank was, even at school. Shit, better check that tape worked.

Martin clatters it into the recorder, rewinds and plays:

'. . . Christ, yes, they all did. I especially remember a piece Frank wrote for the end-of-year magazine our last year at school. It was brilliant, everyone said. The students anyway, the teachers were spitting about it. Remember, Frank?'

'Too long ago for my brain cells, Sid.'

'Something about the immorality of the war. Very controversial at the time. I was quite envious. We were just teenagers you know.'

Great. With luck, there'll be a copy of the article somewhere. But Martin needs to work out the structure of the thing before gathering too much material; the key is in the planning. How do biographers do it?

'Here's your cup of tea, love. I'm just going to pop into town for a bit, get some groceries.'

'Can you give me a lift?'

'Where to?'

'The library.'

Martin runs his finger along the spines of the books following the 800s until he reaches the number memorised from the library computer. *The Art of Biography, The Craft of Biography, Writing Lives, A Question of Biography, Puzzles and Portraits.* He gathers them into his arms like precious fruit and carries them to a desk by the large windows overlooking Civic Square, leaving his bag there to claim the chair.

The biography section seems immense, a forest too great for him to focus on the individual trees. He confines himself to literary biographies, but there are too many. He narrows it further to biographers he knows are good: Richard Ellman, Lytton Strachey, Richard Holmes; subjects he will enjoy: Woolf, Chekhov, Stevenson. Too many, loads too many.

Martin goes back to his desk, sits and counts. Seventeen. He can't take that many out at once. He gets a pen and exercise book from his bag, as two high-school kids come and sit at the table next to him, talking loudly.

'But Mrs Sommers always wants it written that way. You know she won't like it.'

'But don't you think it's good?'

'Of course it's good. But I'm not the one marking it, am I?'

They swing their overloaded bags up on the table, catch Martin's well-directed frown, and lower their voices. Martin takes his pen and heads up a page: Notes. He can't help listening to them.

'Remember at the beginning of term? She made that big long list of things on the blackboard: Essential Qualities Of An Essay. That's practically the only thing she marks on. You have to have all nine qualities, in the right order.'

Martin wonders what the nine qualities are.

'Well I'm not going through my whole life writing essays according to some stupid formula.'

'You don't have to go through your whole life doing it, Jane, just the sixth form.'

They get their books out, whispering now; he can catch only the odd word. Martin looks down into the square and sees a tiny black dog leaping across the grass in front of the art gallery. He opens the first book, reads, flicks through a few pages, reads some more:

It may be pointed out that the biographer and the novelist have many similarities. Both attempt to show life in a true and real sense, despite the fact that one may use imagined events, the other actual ones. While biographers confront the challenge of finding the inner life of their subject, from a collection of events and facts, the novelist may begin from this basis. One can note that novelists use a multitude of ways of intimating a richness through narrative devices, myths, symbols and archetypes, human psychology. The biographer may also make use of these techniques. It's clear that every man creates and refines his own set of private symbols from his own subconscious and the challenge for a biographer is to uncover the fundamental drives in his subject.

Clearly it is an advantage that Martin's subject is still very much alive. He will be able to get inside Frank's mind, follow his thoughts, track the patterns of his unconscious. This book could be useful. He flicks forward.

The key to this relies upon the biographer's motivation. Should he wish to provide a simple chronology only, then the process is relatively straightforward, mainly involving the checking of dates and reliability of his sources. However, should the biographer wish to delve more deeply into the very character and motivations of his subject, we are presented with an ambiguous interaction between the two. Thus the biographer's own character comes under the spotlight, as his motives and judgements have clear implications for the biography that readers may not ignore.

Martin thinks of the Hamilton man also wanting to write Frank's biography. Certainly he's an example of such a case: his motivation will warp his interpretation. Martin will have to be careful to be strictly objective. But he can't believe it's that similar a process to writing fiction. There are always facts to rely upon; there is no uncertainty as to material. He puts the book aside in his maybes pile.

The biographer's duty is to reproduce the truth as closely as he humanly can.

That's more like it. Martin can happily subscribe to that one.

The job of the biographer is to uncover and convey the unobvious truth.

Again, an admirable task. Who could argue against conveying truth? That moment of light when the inner life of the subject is suddenly revealed, exposing the consistency and pattern to the life. That is what he must strive for: the realisation of the meaning of a life. This is what excites him most of all. The question is how to achieve it, how to cast such a light. The truth will not be found in dull facts and statistics, in mere anecdotes and vanities. Where must he look to find the real Frank? What was that quote from Mark Twain? He looks it up.

What a wee little part of a person's life are his acts and his words! His real life is led in his head and is known to none but himself. All day long, and every day, the mill of his brain is grinding, and his thoughts, not those other things, are his history. His acts and his words are merely the visible, thin crust of his world, with its scattered snow summits and its vacant wastes of water – and they are so trifling a part of his bulk! A mere skin enveloping it! The mass of him is hidden – it and its volcanic fires that toss and boil, and never rest, night nor day. These are his life, and they are not written, and cannot be written. Every day would make a whole book of 80,000 words – 365 books a year. Biographies are but the clothes and buttons of the man – the biography of the man himself cannot be written.

Depressing. He puts the book into the no pile, stretches. The schoolgirls have gone; outside the sky is darkening as clouds gather over the harbour. The metallic whales on the bridge across to the waterfront leap up into the rolling grey sea-sky. Martin counts the piles of books: seven definitely not, four maybes and six definite starters. Six are plenty to begin with, he can always come back. He checks his watch. Shit. Alice has been waiting for twenty-five minutes.

A large wine box crouches on the desk like a squatting toad. 'Everything as promised. I thought a wine box was appropriate.' Frank picks out bits and pieces from the cardboard box, holding them up for Martin to admire. 'My grandfather's letters, my father's journal, the family tree compliments of Tom, some of my letters and diaries – I'm still sorting through them, and I've thrown in a couple of early manuscripts too. That should keep you going for a while. Do you want to take away the photo albums too?'

'Might as well. Is there the manuscript of *The Game of the Few*?'
This is what he's most interested in.
'No, couldn't find it, sorry. I'll have another scout around later.'
Martin sets the rock-heavy box down by his chair, discreetly switches the tape recorder on, and registers the number at the top of his notebook. He's got the routine down pat now. He's more sure of Frank too, knows him better, can predict how he'll respond, what gets him going. And plenty does.
'How about we talk some more about your childhood today? Any particular incidents that stand out, that sort of thing.'
Frank is filling his pipe. Flecks of tobacco drop and scatter over the desk like food crumbs. The pipe is integral to Frank.
'When did you first begin smoking?'
'Eh? Well, it weren't when I was a kid, I'll tell you that.'
'Sorry, I was just watching you with the pipe.'
'I've had this pipe must be twenty years. I took up smoking when we moved back to Wellington – no, must've been before that. I can remember smoking a pipe while I wrote editorials at night for the *Nelson Evening Mail*. That must've been about 1970. Shit. No hope for these lungs then.'
'Sorry to get off the track. Go back to your childhood if you like.'
Frank takes his time with the pipe, lighting and puffing, lighting again as it goes out. He sits back, one ankle propped up on the other knee; tilts his head and contemplates the ceiling a while. Martin wonders whether to pause the tape – no, just wait. He quietly pops a sweet into his mouth.
'What's that, boy?'
'Sorry, I'm addicted to aniseed balls. Would you like one?'
He holds the plastic bag up to Frank, who looks at it in wonderment.
'Aniseed balls? I haven't had one of those for years. Good God, I didn't know you could still get them.'
He reaches over a large, calloused hand and puts one in his

mouth, rolling it around his tongue like a cow chewing cud, murmuring appreciatively.

'God that's good.'

A silence of sucking, shattered by a huge guffaw and Frank chokes on the ball, eyes watering, gesturing violently at his back until Martin gets up and thumps him.

'I've got it.'

'You all right?'

'Yes, yes.'

Frank sits again, waves impatiently for Martin to do the same. His eyes are still shining.

'I've got it, a childhood memory. It was the aniseed ball that reminded me. I would have been about nine years old. Yeah, around eight or nine.' He leans back, sucks contentedly on his pipe again and puffs, smiling broadly. 'The time I discovered the difference between boys and girls.'

It sounds like a title.

'I was very much surprised too.'

He laughs in a croak of water draining down gutters.

'It was over at my friend Godfrey's house – we were building a treehouse, if I remember. Yes, a treehouse in the huge puriri out in the front yard. They had a huge section, the Battersbys; it had a long, sweeping driveway round the lawn, and there were lots of large trees along the fence. They even had a tennis court out the back. Very well-to-do, my mother would say. Well, I suppose they were – all that space to run around in. But it was a big, cold house. I remember Mrs Battersby wearing a topcoat inside, it was so cold. Anyway, at the time I'm talking about, we hadn't yet learnt to play tennis and we were busily engaged in the construction of a magnificent treehouse. Maybe we'd read about treehouses in the *Boys' Own Annual*, I don't know, but Mr Battersby had said we could use some old lumber he had in the garage, left over from some project or other. As long as we were very careful, said Mrs Battersby. She was an anxious woman, very pale.'

Martin imagines her standing on the lawn in her topcoat, white face drawn in a worried frown, like his own mother.

'We spent all weekend building that treehouse. I suppose Godfrey's father and older brother did most of the real work, but we were very proud of ourselves at the end of it. We'd hammered in a couple of nails at least. We asked if they would let us sleep in it that night, but they wouldn't. Late in the afternoon, Godfrey's sister Hannah got home. She must've been away for the weekend, I think. She thought the treehouse was marvellous and immediately climbed up into it. But Godfrey and I were still very possessive of our creation and we pushed her out again. Girls weren't allowed, we said. Well, she was a stroppy little sheila, Hannah, and she wasn't having any of that. She kept climbing up and in, until finally Godfrey swore at her and gave her an almighty kick between the legs so she fell right off down to the ground.'

Frank leans forward with his elbows on the desk and looks seriously at Martin, the corners of his lips working.

'I was rather concerned, let me tell you. And not just because she'd run off crying to Mummy, but because I was very capable of imagining what such a kick would have felt like. "You kicked her in the balls!" I said, horrified, to Godfrey. And he laughed and laughed at me. "Girls don't have balls!" he said. "What do you mean?" I said. "They have a slit," he said.'

Puff, puff.

'Well, I remained rather mystified about this for some weeks. I tried to get Godfrey to explain further, but his powers of description weren't up to it. Finally I determined to find out directly. One day I was walking home after school with a few others – Godfrey, Harry Maxwell and Marjorie Hopkins. We were mucking about in the cathedral grounds for a while and I pulled Marjorie into a clump of bushes. She was as cool as a cucumber. "What are you doing, Frank Finnigan?" she said. Well, I said to her, "Do you know that boys and girls are different?" "Of course I do," she said. But she didn't, see. She asked me how different, and I said boys had cocks and girls had slits. "What's a cock?" she said, and I told her, but she didn't believe me; asked me to show her. Well, I said I wouldn't, so she got all interested. Then she tried the old "I'll show you mine if you show me yours".'

He chuckles quietly.

'I was acting smart, holding out a bit, you know. I've always been very good at getting what I wanted. You just have to know what will make someone give it to you. Anyway, I said I'd seen lots of girls before. So then she says she'll give me some aniseed balls from her father's store – they had a store down in the Wood. That was a real bonus, so I said okay, as long as she went first. I still remember the awe I felt as she pulled up her dress and dropped her pants. There it was, this tiny crevice on this lovely smooth whiteness. It didn't last long; she was soon covered up again, demanding I show her mine. I opened up my fly and she still didn't believe me, you know, even with my little cock poking out. She said, "That's just your finger," so I put both my hands over my head and then, Caesar's ghost, did she scream. Godfrey and Harry came running, and for some reason all my courage evaporated and I just took off.'

Martin feels an affinity for the little boy running home. He remembers Lizzie Watson.

'A similar thing happened to me when I was that age.'

'Really? I wonder if everyone has a story like that, then.'

Frank strokes his moustache. 'She told later, of course, but I was able to say she'd been the one to ask me, so I didn't get in too much strife. I never did get those aniseed balls. Funny the things one remembers.'

Chapter 3

'You need to find the assumption the man lives by.'

The sun turns in the sky, a movement so slight, so slow, like a flower growing. Its heat strengthens, reaches out and crawls along Martin's fingers; he holds it in his palm and rocks it gently, a small ball of light, as warm as a secret. He smiles to himself. He is happy today. It is rare, this feeling, and he hugs it to himself with the warmth of the sun, which is already retreating, edging behind an anxious shadow of cloud. His smile twitches, recedes.

He wishes Alice had come to the lunch. It would have helped them get over that fight last night. He feels annoyed again and frowns. She's so damn stubborn. If she'd come she would've seen what Frank was like; she would've understood what he was doing more. She really doesn't have any idea what a biography entails. He shouldn't have told her that though.

Martin stretches his long legs out under the picnic table, draws them up into himself again and sits waiting on the balcony for Frank, his left knee jiggling. There's so much to do, he shouldn't be wasting time like this.

As soon as Frank returns, he asks, 'How about we cover some of your journalism days today?'

'You're keen. I wasn't intending this to turn into a proper session, but okay, as long as we can stay out here.'

Frank sits next to Martin and hands him a beer. They can hear the faint rattle of Connie doing the lunch dishes inside.

'I fished some scrapbooks out for you the other day. Hang

on a tick, I'll get them.'

Frank disappears again and Martin drinks his beer. Maybe he shouldn't have made the suggestion, but hell, they're both relaxed. And Frank's raring to go – all those anecdotes over lunch. He'll just have to remember to write them down.

Martin stirs, reaches down and searches his satchel for pen and paper, finds Alice's grocery list. Alice had been planning on doing the shopping after lunch, but at the last minute another emergency called her back to work. There's always something. Still, Martin thinks he might be relieved; he had been nervous of her and Frank together. He must remember to get the groceries on the way home.

He notices Connie standing just beyond the balcony, indoors.

'Great lunch, Mrs Finnigan.'

He still doesn't feel comfortable calling her Connie. And she still calls him Mr Wrightson, despite Frank objecting each time.

'Good, I'm glad you enjoyed it. Pity your wife could not make it, yes?'

'Yes.'

That sentence structure, second language. She is wavering, a large tulip, bobbing its head in the breeze, waiting for something.

'Maybe next time.'

'You'll be off, then.' She looks at him, eyes as grey as beach pebbles.

Martin wonders whether it is a question, what to say, when Frank appears behind, prodding, arms full of scrapbooks.

'Here we are, here we are. Hey Con, get us some coffee, will you? This may take a while.'

Connie dissolves back into the kitchen. Martin is disquieted, but sees no option. He must talk with Connie soon, interview her; maybe that'd make her more sympathetic to the biography, less . . . what? annoyed? . . . at his growing relationship with Frank? He needs to understand her better too, how she and Frank work.

'This isn't all of them, of course, just a selection. Connie put them together years ago. I couldn't be bothered.'

Frank dumps the pile before Martin, an eager puppy with a heap of chewed shoes, and sits, wagging happily.

'All ready for the instant potted history?'

'Wait a minute.' Martin scuffles again in his satchel and brings out his tape recorder. 'Righty-o, off you go.'

The men smile at each other.

'Where did we get to the other day?'

'You'd left school and tried to enlist.'

'Yeah, well that didn't work, obviously, although plenty of underage ones were still slipping through. When I was refused, my father demanded I either get a job or go back to school. He even made me work in the bakery for a while, but after a few weeks I got fed up with that. Too bloody early in the morning. So I got my first real job, as a messenger and odd-jobs boy at the *Nelson Evening Mail*.'

'When was that?'

'Ah, that would have been the beginning of '42. I was still very keen on going to war, though, and the editor, Fred Spence, he saw that. He kept me reined in tight, made sure I was kept busy – and, I realised later, also made sure I knew all about the newspaper business. They were short-staffed because of the war, so I got roped in to do all sorts of things, even down to helping run the printer. But some days we weren't even allowed to start her up, the newspaper rationing was so bad. We all knew to avoid Mr Spence on those days.'

'What was he like?'

'Fred? He was a newspaper man. He wouldn't suffer fools, and any pomposity got short shrift. He was always patient with me, though, always had a twinkle in his eye. He taught me to type, two-fingered style, and started grooming me to be a reporter. Straightforward, clean copy, that's what he liked. Not like that shit that gets through nowadays. I started off at my own volition doing weekend reporting, to get a leg in. Eventually I got on the reporting staff by default. After I'd been there a year they began sending me off to cover court with another reporter. I thought I was the bee's knees, sitting there in court with all the lawyers, scribbling away in my notebook. Shocking copy, of course, shocking. Hah. But I greatly enjoyed myself, even if most of the crime was petty stuff – theft, assaults, that sort of thing.'

Martin can see Connie out the corner of one eye. She's doing something by the balcony doors. She often seems to be fiddling about on the sidelines, eavesdropping; he'd rather she came straight out and sat down with them to listen.

'So you didn't get any training?'

'No. Not like today, with all these journalism schools. I don't know what the hell they teach them. I think reporting today is a damned disgrace. No, I was entirely self-taught. The subs soon pulled me up if I was running off the rails. Actually I don't know why they started me off on court, that's the most dangerous reporting of the lot. But it seemed to be a tradition: start the young ones off in the deep end. I was on with another man, Billy someone or other, but all the same. I always thought it a dangerous system, because you can make a mistake or say something libellous and get the paper in a lot of trouble. I seem to remember I did make a fairly serious mistake once . . . what was that? Maybe it was mixing up the defendant's and the victim's names or something.'

'So how long were you at the *Mail*?'

'Till '44. I still had itchy feet you see, kept seeing those army ads: you know the ones, "The Spirit of Anzac Calls You, Enlist Now for Overseas Service." I was determined to do my duty, though Mr Spence wasn't happy. I eventually managed to sign up when I was seventeen. The war was practically over by then, of course. The Americans had come into it years before, and by then the bastards were well on the run.'

Frank's on a roll.

'They sent me up to a camp at Featherston in the Wairarapa,

where a whole lot of country boys were living in tents and huts, being trained up. There was a lot of foot slogging, but we all regarded it as a bit of adventure. Of course by then plenty of our boys had been killed as well, so we knew it wasn't all fun and games, but there was a kind of distance to it, you know, a kind of unreality. They kept us there about nine months before we finally got on a boat. No one was quite sure where we were off to, I don't think. There were various suggestions. I guess the bosses didn't even know, because Germany surrendered when we were in the middle of the Pacific Ocean and we were left floating around wondering what to do with ourselves. All that bloody training and not a bit of action! Still, I was glad to be out of New Zealand, away from my family. Eventually they sent us on to Britain, and after that the bomb was dropped and it really was all over.'

'So you never saw any action?'

'Sorry, boy. No war hero I.'

'Do you have diaries that cover those years?'

'Could do. Might be ones for '44 and '45 anyway – I definitely remember writing one in camp. A few letters should be there somewhere at least.'

Martin clears the scrapbooks to the side of the wobbly table as Connie comes out with coffee and milk.

'No biscuits?' asks Frank.

'There aren't any.'

Martin feels distinctly told off. She doesn't want him here, that's clear. But there's something more – some tension between her and Frank that's not to do with him. At least he doesn't think it is. He should observe their relationship more closely. He has assumed too much, assumed they follow the patterns of their generation; but perhaps it's not that simple.

Martin smiles apologetically. 'We won't be much longer.'

But Connie's already gone and Frank's waving a hand in the air. Two baubles of coffee cling to his moustache, tiny Christmas decorations on a bristling grey fir tree.

'Take as long as you like, I wasn't planning any work this afternoon anyway.' He slurps his coffee. 'I'm bloody sure there are biscuits.'

He stomps off to find them.

Martin opens one of the scrapbooks and peers at the thin columns of yellowing type. 1947. The clippings are from the *Evening Post*: Borough Council reports, a Plunket Society meeting, an Agricultural and Pastoral show at Lower Hutt. The tiered headlines seem tiny by today's standards, and the type harder to read. He reaches 1949 just as Frank comes back, triumphant.

'You see! Chocolate even. I'm starting to worry about Connie's memory. Ah, you're on to the *Post*. Let's have a look. We used to cover everything that moved in those days. The squeak of the old parish pump, you know.'

Frank's large hands latch on to the scrapbook. Laughter belches forth and the table shakes.

'Look at this, boy. Papers used to be so damn prim and proper when I was first in journalism. This article about a parliamentary paper on VD – and I wasn't even allowed to mention the word! See this, it says, "the social complaint". Hah. Social complaint. I usually did the council round, and sometimes I filled in at court. See this tax evasion case – all this fuss recently, well, it's nothing new. It was going on in Sid Holland's day. Mind you, I remember most income tax was only about four pounds then.'

He settles back down into his too-small chair, and the seat creaks ominously.

'This one, this was the first hanging I went to. The first, and last. This bloke Metcalf battered his wife to death with an iron, but no one believed him for a while, you know, things like that just didn't happen. Hangings were becoming less common by then, but journalists were still invited to attend, as witnesses as well as reporters. If you didn't want to, you could be excused on conscience grounds. But I agreed, I'm a gallows man. Tom Long, the hangman, got paid twenty-five pounds per hanging.'

'What was it like?'

'What was it like? It was like a hanging. Haul him up, kick the support, snap, that's it. Sometimes took a few minutes. Still, better than that electric chair they use in America. Did you read someone's head caught fire on that the other day? Now that is barbaric.'

'Did you enjoy journalism?' Martin is about to tell him that he almost went into journalism himself, but resists, afraid Frank may laugh.

'Yeah, I guess I did. I was never really a newspaper man at heart, though. I could see how I could have become one, you know – sometimes the adrenalin really got you. I still think it's a bloody important job, if it's done right. People need to have the facts; they need to know what's going on in the world and why, and it's the media's job to tell them. I'm not sure they do any more. It's all bloody television today, all sound bites and celebrities, it's pathetic. That's not news. Where are the facts? Just the straight facts? The reader needs to have all the facts available to them so they can make up their own minds, not get spoon-fed someone else's opinions. What we need is the reader in control.'

'What about in fiction? The reader's not in control then.'

Frank leans forward into the sun, a gleam in his eye, and for a minute Martin thinks he's going to take him by the hand.

'Ah, that's where you're wrong, boy. I've learnt that the hard way. I used to think that in my fiction it was me in control: it was the author dictating to the reader, if you like. The reader may have been a willing participant, but it was always the author who had the final say. That's a good feeling, omnipotence. That could be what drives all writers.'

He shifts back again into shadow. A pulse is tapping above Martin's left eyebrow.

'But I'm not so sure of that any more. I've had thousands of readers, right, thousands. They've all read exactly the same story, but they all come away with something different. I'm constantly astonished by it, the way readers will believe something is in a story when it's not, or the way they pick up on different aspects, peculiar to them. It's incredible. It's like ten people witnessing the same crime – a bank robbery, say – and remembering ten different versions of the same event. Some will give a different order of events; some will misremember the clothes the robbers were wearing; and one person will even describe something that never happened at all.'

'But surely . . .'

'No, I tell you, boy, I've become convinced that the reader's experience is very different from that of the writer, and why not just as valid? After all, their minds are working on the same material, but in a different way. Who am I to say their interpretation, their meaning, if you like, isn't real, isn't true?'

The phone is ringing in the distance. A bird in a tree echoes the trill.

'So you . . . you're almost arguing "Death of the Author" you know, Frank. Didn't you say my thesis was, quote, a load of bollocks, close quote?'

'Well it was. But the concept does appeal to me in a way.'

The phone is still ringing; there's no sign of Connie. Frank gets up and lumbers inside to answer the call. When he returns, he's frowning, his craggy white eyebrows frozen, poised to crash in an avalanche of ice.

'Bloody children. Anyway.' He sits. 'We were talking about journalism.'

Martin wants to resume the fiction strand of the conversation, but the eyebrows warn him to leave it there, dangling. He tugs at the thread a little.

'So do you think the reader performs the same role in journalism?'

'The reader? Hacks don't take much notice of readers. They just go out and do their job, and once it's written it's on to the next story. Anyway, journalism is all about facts. People tend to believe it. Listen, Martin, do you fancy going down to the pub?'

He checks his watch. Nearly four already. 'I really should get going, Frank.'

'Nah, come on, just one pint at the local. Connie seems to have gone out. She won't mind. What do you say? I'd like to introduce you to a friend of mine. Bound to be there at this time.'

The friend is tempting.

'I'll just have to ring Alice.'

'Sure, sure. Come on.'

Frank's local is grubby. Not the sort of place Martin would choose to drink in. A few men sit, either alone or in pairs, on tall stools at sticky Formica tables, glassily staring at the racing channel. Smoke hangs in the air, coats the patrons in a blurry aura. Martin stands uncertainly behind Frank, who is at the bar ordering pints. He feels like an eighteen-year-old invited by his father to a pub for the first time.

They go and sit at a table. Martin tries to push the sash window up without much success, but at least a faint breeze steals in through the gap.

'So where's your friend?'

'Harry? Yeah, where is Harry?' Frank glances round the room, then turns back to his beer. 'Can't be here yet. Won't be long.'

Martin feels duped. 'I hope not. I can't stay too long, you know, Frank.'

'Never mind that, boy. Settle down, the race is about to begin.'

'Do you come here often?'

'Often enough.'

'Does Connie mind?'

Frank glances over at him, gulps a third of a pint in one swallow, then turns back to the horses.

'Glad to get me out of the house. Gives her a chance to do her own stuff. Here see, number three, Finnigan's Wake, beautiful, ten dollars on the nose.'

'Her own stuff?'

'Yeah, poetry mainly. You should read some. She's pretty good. Here we are, she likes a wet track – see, she's up there all right . . . Go for it.'

Martin shifts on his stool as Frank watches the race. He sips his pint and wonders how soon he can leave. If only this friend would turn up.

'Bugger! Can you believe it? They've got to appeal. She did good though, eh boy. Did you see that?'

'Yeah, shame. So, who is this Harry?'

'God, I can't believe it.'

Frank sits back down on his stool, draws on his pint.

'Harry? I met Harry when I first went to Hong Kong in '51, freelancing. That was a great time – hard yacker, though; the real stories were only just coming out about the red tide in '49. Fucking communists.'

Martin wonders if he should bring out his tape recorder, decides against it.

'I first met Harry at the FCC, the Foreign Correspondents Club. She was a real beauty. They pulled it down later – typical bloody Hong Kong, nothing's ever left as it is. They were a great group of journos there then. We'd all sit round the bar each night, comparing stories – you never liked to think someone had something you didn't, you know. People would keep the good stuff pretty close to their chests, but you could always tell if someone had something, and we'd always get it out of them by the end of the night.'

'So you'd co-ordinate stories amongst yourselves?'

'We'd share information, that's all. Everyone benefited and we all got our stories straight.'

'Seems like collusion to me.'

'No, no, no, Jesus. You know nothing about it. It was just pooling resources. That way your readers were most likely to get the whole truth.'

'Or only one version of the truth.'

Frank downs the rest of his pint in disgust, moves off to go to the toilet. Martin sits, frowning at his own half-empty glass, sips a bit more. When Frank comes back he has two fresh pints in his hands.

'You still haven't told me who Harry is.'

Frank's grinning at something behind Martin. His hand rises in a wave.

'This, my boy, this is Harry.'

Martin turns on the stool, and his gaze jolts down to a short, slight Chinese man who is grinning back at Frank.

'Harry Ling, meet Martin Wrightson.' Frank pulls up another stool. 'Let me get you a beer, Harry.'

'No, no, Mr Finnigan. I get it.'

Harry goes to the bar and Martin looks at Frank.

'So, that's Harry.'

'That's Harry. Me old mate from the FCC.'

'Who was he a correspondent for?'

Frank roars. 'He was the bloody barman, Martin.'

Harry returns with three more dripping pints and sets them down expertly on the snail-sticky table. He nods at them, and raises one of the foaming mugs.

'Cheers.'

'Cheers.'

They all drink. It's more bitter than Martin's used to.

'I was just telling Martin about the old Hong Kong days, Harry.'

'Oh, yes. The old days. All gone now, eh, Frank Finnigan.'

'Yeah, it's all different now, all right, Harry. I went back a few years ago, Martin, me and Connie, just for a week or so. Very Chinese, hardly a sign of the Brits being there at all, even then.'

'What did you think of the handover?'

'All those fireworks? A lot of bloody fuss over nothing. Old

Chris Patten with a tear in his eye as the Union Jack falls – what a lot of bloody nonsense. You want to know what I think? I think the Brits are a pack of fucking hypocrites, that's what I think. All that palaver about the threat to democracy and how you can't trust those commie bastards over the border. What bullshit. The media were just lapping it up, of course, believing anything they're told. Hong Kong never had democracy! The Brits ruled it for all those years through governors; it was only practically in the last few weeks before they had to hand it back that Patten suddenly makes all this big deal about giving them democracy. What a lot of crap. To say the Chinese aren't fit to rule it, when it's their own bloody country to start with, what bollocks. Makes me spit.'

'What do you think, Harry?'

Harry is sitting there quietly, beer in one hand, that little grin still on his sun-circle face.

'A lot of people worried, eh, but me, I'm not worried. I'm a Kiwi now. I live here since 1966. My friend, Frank Finnigan, he help me get here and I won't go back to Hong Kong. Too many people, eh? And those Chinese, can't trust those Chinese, eh?' He laughs.

'Old Chinese they say, "Kill the chicken to scare the monkeys."'

Both Frank and Harry lift up their heads and laugh, a booming guffaw punctuated by an odd quacking noise. Martin laughs quietly too, though he has no idea at what.

'If they'd really been concerned about it, the Brits could've done something years ago. Even back when I was first there, Hong Kong's future was being discussed. You remember that *Daily Telegraph* guy, Harry?'

'Three Gin Gerry.'

'Yeah, that's the one. I'd forgotten that. Three Gin Gerry. Had balls on him like a scoutmaster. Anyway, he was a great admirer of Clement Attlee, the British Labour leader. Remember how delighted he was when Attlee won the election, Harry? Of course, as soon as Attlee came to power the Brits decided to give up extraterritoriality. I talked to British friends in the Governor's office at great length about it and even tried to write a story, but no one was very interested. I couldn't believe Britain was serious in giving up all its territories, and I was asking why they didn't take the opportunity to renew their lease on Hong Kong then. China was over the moon at the Brits giving up their territorial rights just like that, and they stood a bloody good chance of renewing their lease on the New Territories at the time. Besides, Honkers was tiddlywinks to the Chinese then.' Frank leans over Martin and raises one large bristling beetle of an eyebrow. 'The answer I got, and I still remember it to this day, was that 1997 was a long way away, and besides it would be too much trouble.'

Harry's and Frank's incongruous laughs merge again.

'Of course no one ever said that on the record.'

Martin smiles and checks his watch. Alice.

'I must go.'

'Just get us another beer first, eh?'

Martin opens the bedroom door cautiously, but the light is on and Alice is sitting up in bed, reading. A bad sign.

'Oh, hi. You're still up.'

'Just reading. I gave up on TV about ten, shortly after I gave up on you.'

'Sorry, Alice. I did ring you.'

She always gets him defensive like this. Martin stops himself from pointing out that if she'd come to the lunch in the first place, they both would have been home a lot earlier.

'Yes, you did ring me. And each call was progressively drunker.'

'We did go get something to eat. Eventually.'

Martin resents her smiling at him. Cow. He concentrates on pulling off his shoes and socks. His feet seem oddly long and white. He picks at a callus on his little toe. He's getting old.

'Why don't you come to bed instead of staring at your feet?'

'I'm coming, I'm coming.'

No doubt she'll complain about the beery breath too. He goes into the bathroom to brush his teeth.

'We went to Frank's local,' he calls.

'Yes, I know. You told me.'

Martin washes his face. The face cloth is soft and warm, and he presses it against his eyes a minute. It's blood-warm. He sways and holds on to the sink with one hand to steady himself. As long as he doesn't throw up, it'll be fine. He goes to the toilet for another piss. He hasn't drunk this much in a long time – not since he was a student, probably. Frank can sure hold his liquor. Maybe he's alcoholic? Maybe that's the secret. But Harry seemed to have no trouble keeping up with him. Must be all those years of being a bartender. Nice fellow, Harry. He would have told him a lot more about Frank; but Frank wouldn't give him a chance, and when Harry went to the bar once Frank whispered that Harry was 'a few bricks short of a load'. It didn't seem like it.

'You all right in there?'

'Just coming.'

Alice is still sitting up, smiling at him, her old jersey – baby-bootee pink – over her nightie. He remembers fumbling up that pink woolly jersey before they were married, and smiles back at her. She's lovely really. She looks after him.

'Come to bed then, Goofy.'

He gets in and rests his head against hers, his lips next to her ear.

'Sorry, Ali.'

'That's all right, honey.'

'I think I drank too much.'

'I know. That's all right too.' She pushes him back slightly so she can look at his face. 'I've been thinking, I'm going to have to resign myself to you having an affair.'

'What?' Martin bolts up and clasps her hands. 'No, no. I've been with Frank!'

Alice giggles. Her face as round as an orange. 'I know, Martin. That's who I mean.'

He must have drunk more than he'd realised. He's all wobbly bobbly.

'What?'

'It's like an affair. To write this biography, you're going to have to spend a lot of time with Frank, you're going to have to know him intimately. Whether you end up loving or hating him, you're going to have to know him better than you know me. Better than he knows himself. See? You're going to have to be married to him for a while.'

Marry Frank?

'I think you're taking this night of drinking together a li'l' too seriously, Alice.'

She laughs again, her teeth tiny white unyielding crags.

'I'll still make time for you and Lance, I promise.'

Poor little Lance. He hasn't seen enough of the boy lately. Just like his own father – always busy, always away working. He'd promised himself he wouldn't be like that. Martin's eyes prickle with tears.

'It's okay, Martin. I'm not too worried about it. I've just been thinking about what you're really doing. You're writing someone's life. It's a huge thing.'

'Yeah. That's what I've been trying to tell you.'

He thinks of Frank, that loud guffaw, the puffs of smoke: what are they hiding?

Huge. She has no idea.

'This biography of Byron that John gave me to read made me think about it. You need to really know him, know his motives as much as you know your own.'

John again. Fucking John, what does he know?

Martin doesn't like the way she's started quoting John. The

man talks a load of codswallop. From arsehole to breakfast table, as Frank would say. He settles back against the pillow, lightly closes his eyes. A mistake. He quickly opens them again and anchors his vision on the light amid the rotating ceiling.

'You need to find the assumption the man lives by,' Alice persists.

Martin closes his eyes again.

The spinning might as well be black.

'Okay, hon. I'll turn off the light now. Night.'

He feels her smooth lips brush his cheek. It's like the soft fluttering of a moth's wings. Large, soft wings of dust, flapping, covering his face and lifting again, covering and lifting with each breath: inhale, exhale. Inhale. Exhale.

Martin doodles around the edges of his list of interview subjects; the phone droops limply in his other hand, burring at him. He hangs up and sighs. All the easy ones are done and the others are impossible to get hold of. He slowly sketches a koru, a lifeline spiralling inwards, clutching its meaning close to its chest. Martin hums softly to it, drawing it out, an unfurling fern frond. He listens to it bristling. He feels Lance come up behind him, the boy's soft breath against his arm as he shades in the fern. The teacher had said Lance was good at art. Martin turns to his son, holding out the sheet of paper like a tray of biscuits.

'Would you finish it for me?'

He's rewarded by an eager smile – he hasn't seen so many of those lately – and the boy gallops off just as the phone shrieks. It's for Alice. As usual. He calls her and goes back into his study.

The blue folder lies open on his desk. Lists of lists, lines of names and numbers. Martin smiles and sits. He's crossed off the publishing company after speaking to them early this morning. He isn't sure he impressed them terribly, but they've agreed to have a look at the first draft, so that's something. No deadlines either; he's been worrying about that. Who else is on the list? He managed to get hold of Joseph Levy this morning too, and he was pretty good value. Doesn't know anything about literature, of course, but he seems to know Frank pretty well. Anyway, he can tick off another name. Martin takes up his red pen, deliberately scars the white flesh of the margin by pressing the ink in two exact blood strokes. It feels as good as a death.

He puts the list of interviews to one side and opens up the list of hard copy material he needs to find. That old school yearbook, for instance, which Sid Hewlitt mentioned. It could be useful to slot some of his early school writings into chapter three. Maybe the magazine's among that school stuff Frank gave him.

Martin goes to hunt through one of the boxes lined up chronologically against the far wall. Exercise books, text books, drawings, photos; here's an old tin of cough drops, some magazines – here we are, Nelson College 1942, that's what . . . 15. Fifth form roll, yes: Francis Finnigan, George Garthwaite, Edward Gilpin, Sid Hewlitt. The index lists articles by senior students Louis Duncan, Richard Baigent, Terry Marshall and . . . Sid Hewlitt. No Frankie. But Sid, that's odd. Page 18: 'The immorality of warfare: an argument against New Zealand's involvement in the Second World War', by Sid Hewlitt. What . . .

He's read about something like this in that book Frank lent him on biographies: the subjectivity of memory. Yeats: *It must be that I have changed many things without my knowledge.* Bizarre. Great men's contemporaries remember greatness in their adolescence that did not exist, perhaps. But such a mistake, when he wrote it himself!

Martin puts the yearbook on his desk and stares at the cover. He can't cope with this yet.

Alice is calling him to the phone. One of his interview subjects has finally got back. He goes eagerly, happy for the distraction, and talks to the man for half an hour, though he only knew Frank slightly and really has nothing to add. After hanging up, he sits and looks at the list of names again. Some he can't quite categorise, and others Frank can't – or won't – find contacts for. That French woman, there was something about her. The other day he'd found a letter from her amidst the pile – it wasn't particularly interesting, he'd asked Frank about her, only idly. Martin had thought she was German first of all, with that name, Lerner. But Frank had said a French journalist, Agence France-Presse.

Martin reaches for the phone book and looks her up. No listing. And he can't find AFP. Think, investigative – try French, try the Alliance Française. He looks up that number, humming.

He has to pretend he's the son of an old friend before they will give it to him, and is shocked when the woman answers his call.

'Elena Lerner?'

'Oui. Who is there?'

'My name is Martin Wrightson, I'm writing a biography of Frank Finnigan.'

A brief silence. He should have prepared.

'I've been told not to talk to you,' she says. The click in his ear sounds like a kiss.

Martin stands up indignantly, his fist clenched around the receiver. Alice, coming into the hall, sees his expression.

'Martin?'

'I'm going out.'

He grabs his keys and a jacket and strides out the front door, only to turn and stride back. He's forgotten his tape recorder.

The glass door opens. She is quite beautiful for her age, grey hair elegantly whipped into a bun. Her long neck, though softened and loose with age, is still seductive.

'Monsieur Wrightson.'

He is caught off guard, expecting her to be.

'Mrs Lerner.'

'I'm not going to talk to you.'

Anger flows again, strengthening, and he swallows it gratefully.

'Who told you not to? Did Frank?'

'Pas de personne. Nobody told me not to. I made that up.'

Somehow he believes her. Her eyes are purple; he can smell lavender.

'Why?'

'Because I can't be bothered talking to you. I don't want to, there's no point.'

'But it's not about you, it's about Frank.'

'Exactement.'

'But you're an old friend of his, aren't you? You've known him a long time, you must be able to give me some useful material.'

She laughs, a young laugh, just a slight rattle towards the end. 'I'm sure I can, darlink, but I won't. It is not material, it is my life. Besides . . .' She leans against the doorway and takes a cigarette from her pocket, lights it. '. . . I've forgotten most of it.'

She puffs smoke at him. If only he can get her to take him inside.

'Okay, I won't interview you. But what if you just showed me some photos, some old letters maybe?'

Elena straightens up, her face tightening, eyes sharp.

'It is not possible. I have burnt them.'

She turns and closes the door behind her, as if he has been the one to end the meeting, as if he is halfway down the road already.

'So these are all from when you were in the Press Gallery?'

Martin is bent over, shuffling through a box of scrapbooks at his feet. He spreads some out on the lounge floor.

'Yep, that's all from the Gallery, after I got back from overseas. I got the job at the Press Association in '54. I'd been filing copy to AAP from Hong Kong, so I knew agency journalism by then. The Press Gallery was something new, though. Bloody politics. It hasn't changed, you know, nothing has.'

Martin reads some of the articles on various parliamentary reports and speeches.

'It looks fairly dry stuff.'

'Dry? That's real reporting, boy. Accurate. Comprehensive. None of these beat-ups or personality politics you see today.'

'I thought you said nothing's changed.'

'Well, the reporting's changed. Personality politicking still went on back then, you know. Nash and Holyoake, all them, they weren't pure. But reporters stayed out of it, see, we stuck to the facts. The public don't want to know all that bullshit anyway. They don't want to know what Bill Clinton did with some tart. That's not the issue. It's bloody outrageous.'

'So which party did you support?'

'Which party? I'm neither right nor left. I'm correct. Back then I had friends in both parties, but I never voted; prided myself on being non-partisan, strictly fair. That was the good thing about PA. Some of the papers – well, they were owned by members of the National Party, like *The Dominion*. PA, though – I never once had any interference with my copy.'

'Did other reporters?'

'I don't really know, boy. You heard the odd story. In the Gallery, though, once you were there you were regarded as pretty senior and the subs didn't touch you much. There were only ten or so print reporters in the Gallery in my day: two from PA, two from *The Post*, *The Dom*, *The Herald* and one bloke who represented the *Christchurch Press* and the *ODT*. We were thorough all right. Nowadays bills in the House get hardly a bloody inch of copy. They don't even report MPs' maiden speeches. Used to be the best part of a page devoted to Parliament. It was reported in much more detail than today. A speech would get three-quarters of a column, when now it gets only a few lines.'

'Maybe the speeches are worse today?'

'Well there could be something in that. We didn't pay too much attention to merit. Us PA reporters had to work like dogs. We had to cover all the parliamentary sessions. There was no overtime either. If the House sat till 3am, we sat till 3am. Les and I would share the work, one watching the House while the other wrote stories, and the boy from the office would come down to get the copy. Those lazy bastards from the other papers would sneak round too sometimes and take carbon copies off ours.'

'I suppose you used shorthand.'

'Shorthand? Come off it. I suppose I used a bastardised kind of shorthand, though, my own code. Those old typewriters too, you really had to bash the keys down. None of these fancy computers then. If I had to use spellcheck I'd commit suicide. We typed stories up in the gallery overlooking the debating chamber, all the reporters in one office, and we ate with the MPs in Bellamy's dining room. I was on a first-name basis with most of them. Nash would talk to me sometimes – he was underrated, I reckon. Holyoake was okay. Once he got in, though, he suddenly had no time for us. Pompous little man.'

'What do you think of politicians today?'

'Mad as fucking maggots. Every one of them. This MMP system, it's buggered it right up. You've got every Tom, Dick and Hori in there now. All those Maoris, demanding money for land that was taken hundreds of years ago and now belongs to law-abiding taxpayers like you and me. Any bastard calling me a Pakeha is likely to get a fist down his throat.'

Connie comes in and nearly trips over a scrapbook. She glares at the carpet of newsprint and frowns at Frank.

'What did I say?'

'What? Oh, yeah, all right, don't go crook. Let's go downstairs, eh Marty?'

They troop downstairs, Martin feeling shamefaced, like a boy told to clean up his toys. In the study, Frank opens the french doors and the fresh cold morning air brightens his eyes. Martin starts to get out the scrapbooks again.

'Ah, put them away. You can look at them later.'

Frank sits on the doorstep, feet outside, and lights his pipe. Martin reluctantly puts the swollen scrapbooks away. He must read them thoroughly later; they help place Frank in the past.

'So what do you think of these articles now?'

Frank looks up at him and puffs. His eyes look very blue.

'I think it was good work. I think it was honest.' He turns back outside. 'Maybe I should have stuck to being a newspaper man.'

'You say that as if you don't think what you do now is honest.'

Frank doesn't turn round. A bird in one of the trees is ringing like a bell. He's losing him. Martin remembers something Alice said the other night.

'What is the assumption you live by, Frank?'

Frank leans back, looks up, surprised, more open. Martin can see him thinking about it. There's a silence for a while, and Martin asks the question of himself. He doesn't want to answer. Maybe Frank doesn't either. But he's taking the pipe from his mouth, looking at him as if he's his father, trying to explain something important, like death.

'I think . . . that there is always more to do, that you can always do better.' He looks perplexed, as if he hasn't quite got it. 'That what I've done is not good enough.'

Something tightens in Martin's throat. If someone with so much success can feel that way, surely . . . No. He won't let Frank feel that way. He waves agitatedly at the bookshelves, the pile of clippings on the table.

'But look . . .'

Frank is turning away again, so Martin snatches a scrapbook up from the floor and waves it under his nose.

'All this . . .'

But Frank's puffing out into the garden, watching two birds dance around a piece of bread on the lawn. Martin is left squatting uncomfortably beside him, disconsolately flipping through the scrapbook, his eyes glazed, unseeing.

'Wait a minute.'

Something has caught Frank's eye. He's taking the scrapbook in one hand, pointing to a picture of a ship listing heavily in rough seas, tilted over on one side like a teapot gone awry.

'Look at this.'

He shows Martin the story accompanying. **THEY'LL NOT FORGET THE CRUEL SEA** shouts the headline. It's the *Wahine*.

'Now this, this was one of the reasons I left journalism. This was one of the saddest stories of my life.'

Chapter 4

'Now this, this was one of the saddest stories of my life.'

Even Martin remembers the day that became known as Wahine Day. He was five years old and was woken before dawn by a howling wind battering his bedroom window. Living in Karori, on the western hills behind Wellington Harbour, he was a boy well-used to the wind's voice. But this was different, this felt like an animal beating against the walls, and for the first time in two proud years he wet his bed.

Martin reads the beginning of the Evening Post news story, dated 11 April 1968. A large black headline thunders **THEY'LL NOT FORGET THE CRUEL SEA.**

As a cold, misty dawn broke over the Eastern Bays this morning, a convoy of Army trucks made their way home around the coast stacked with laden coffins – a grim reminder of yesterday's Wahine disaster.

'Did you write this?'

Frank nods.

'Something of it anyway. Me and two other blokes. We all started on the Seatoun side, but a lot of the survivors washed over the other side of the harbour too. I've never seen anything like it. I can still see their faces, such haggard, grey faces, as they staggered in from the sea. Still see those faces at night sometimes.'

It was a cold dawn, but a welcome one. For it brought with it the much-needed light that the searchers had been without through the long hours of the night. More than 80 members of the police, Army and Federated Mountain Club and local residents combined to comb the beaches in the all-night search for bodies from the tragedy.

'Tell me what it was like.'

Martin clatters a tape into the recorder and switches on the play button in his excitement. One of Frank's tales suddenly booms around the room: ' . . . and there was one of those JC birds walking over the water . . .' He swears softly and turns it off again, fumbling with the record button.

'Aren't you going to keep that?'

'I've transcribed it already. Don't worry. Tell me about the *Wahine*.'

Frank moves away from the windows and stands by the bookshelf for a while. Martin is about to prompt him again when he exclaims and pulls out a book.

'Read this.' He hands it to him. 'It's by the other two journos who were with me. That'll tell you what it was like.'

'But I want you to tell me.' A child, whining. 'Please.'

Frank sits down heavily behind the desk and rubs his eyes.

'All right. But turn that thing off.'

Martin is aghast. Frank looks up and almost smiles, the snowy clumps of his eyebrows rising negligibly: a slight shift of landscape.

'I will tell you first, and . . .' He waves disparagingly at the tape recorder. '. . . I'll tell that thing later.'

It seems the only way. Martin leans forward and reluctantly turns off the machine. A tiny river of panic runs through him. He sits washed up on the chair and listens.

'It was an unbelievable day. Do you remember it?'

Martin thinks of the howling wind wolves and nods.

'I woke up about 6 am that day. There was a Godawful noise outside and the bedroom curtains were flying up to the ceiling, even though the windows were all shut. We lived on Alexandra Road then, up round Mount Victoria and Roseneath, looking out to the south. I didn't know it, but the real drama was already going on out near the harbour entrance as the ferry tried to battle its way in. Our daughter, Nancy, she was about ten, she came running into the bedroom saying the lounge windows were wobbling, so I jumped out and went to look and, my God, these huge big picture windows were bending in and out like this.'

Frank flaps his arms like wings.

'I closed the curtains and told the children to stay in the north-facing rooms, away from the windows. We were scared of glass going everywhere. Behind us there was a house up top, and we could see bits of its roof peeling off – and sheets of iron taking off, luckily the other way. There were trees falling over all about us and everything in the garden was getting absolutely shredded. By the end of the day there wasn't anything – no leaves left on any of the trees, those big soft-leafed native trees, you know, just totally bloody shredded. So it was a fucking frightening day.'

Martin nods, not wanting to interrupt. Frank tells a good story.

'The power was off, I remember, but we had a little transistor. It kept fading in and out because the batteries were almost flat, you know how it is. Being short of money we didn't have any spares. I've never forgotten what it's like not to have money. Anyway, about half past seven, I think it was, we heard the *Wahine* was in trouble and I said to Connie, "I've got to go to work".

'I went in to the newsroom, which was in Brandon House then, and there were about five or six people on. Everyone was phoning around. It looked like it was going to be a busy enough day for us anyway, what with the winds already wreaking havoc around the region, and I remember someone cursing "more bloody weather stories". Hah. This was going to be the biggest "bloody weather story" of them all.'

Martin can see Frank's eyes glassing over. It's as if he's talking to himself.

'I remember later talking to the NZBC reporter who broke the news – what was her name? Carol someone, she'd got a call from a Marine Department official. Jesus, that was the greatest news tip in the history of New Zealand journalism! He told her the *Wahine* had grounded on a shoal near Barretts Reef and some of their men had gone out to have a look. She checked with the Harbour Board tolls office and the wharf police, and had it confirmed just before seven. I must have heard one of the first bulletins about it.'

'PA didn't get a lot at first. As the morning went on they kept downplaying it. The radio was running the same stories too, police saying there was "no serious danger". I guess it did look for a while as if she'd be okay. After she hit the rocks, they managed to anchor and began drifting into the harbour. Still seemed pretty damned dangerous to me, this huge bloody ship swinging back and forth in this hurricane, each time just missing those jagged rocks. Have you been up there? Those rocks are bloody vicious. I was sure she was a goner. I remember saying so to Mack Lambert and we decided to get out there. There was nothing more to be got from ringing round the authorities, and they were busy with their own crises. We left the other reporters to write up the stories of floods and falling trees, roofs being ripped off, slips and so on. It was really one out of the box.

'It made it a hell of a struggle to even get out to Seatoun. When we finally got to the top of the hill road leading from Miramar to Worser Bay the area had been sealed off by police and council staff. This was about 12.30, I guess. This prick of a man wouldn't let us through, kept saying orders were orders and he had specific instructions to let through nothing but emergency rescue vehicles. We kept arguing, but the guy said we would need a signed letter from the Commissioner of Police before we could get through. So we tried another way. There were so many cars on the road we had to drive up on the footpath and go like that. Some drivers had simply abandoned their cars in the middle of the road while they watched what was going on in the bay. We got out at one point to look, and it was simply unbelievable. This huge great ferry bobbing around like an iceblock being shaken in a glass. It was listing by then too, shuddering and slowly tipping. We watched the tugboat backing up to the stern and trying to catch a couple of lines which the ferry was firing out, but they all missed. The winds were beginning to ease slightly by then, and we thought we better get down there, in case they abandoned ship.

'We eventually managed to slip down a road leading to Seatoun, planning to drive from there round to the bay, but there was another bloody roadblock and another fuckwit traffic officer. We tried to flash our press passes but it was no dice. I was going berserk by then, so I simply put my foot down and drove on to the footpath and past the block, with this guy running alongside screaming blue murder.' Frank guffawed so loudly it caught in his throat, and he had to stop to cough it out.

'What happened then?'

'Well, we got to the coast and you could see they were abandoning ship. Three of the life boats had been lowered in already and crew were throwing over the life rafts, some of which inflated okay, but others just seemed to blow away, or inflate upside down. Now and then through the horizontal rain we could make out little figures leaping from the ship straight into the sea. It all seemed very unreal. Mack took off one way and I went the other, and we got busy, asking people on the beach about it, but they knew as much or as little as we did and it quickly became ridiculous to be asking questions, so I offered to help. I guess it was the first time I'd really got involved with a story.

'Some guys were trying to launch an outboard motorboat from the slipway near Seatoun Wharf, but it was impossible. The seas were still enormous, crashing over the slip and rocks. They went round to Worser Bay instead and I think they got in okay from there. I went round to the Boating Club where people were gathering, debating what to do. You could see the *Aramoana* heading down the harbour and the boaties were scoffing she'd be no use, the life rafts would simply be dashed to death against her. There were lots of little boats going out, people had poured into the bay, a lot had come straight from their city offices to help, and there were all these men in suits and ties heading these little boats, like a corporate armada.

'By this time a general message had gone out that passengers were abandoning the *Wahine* and all available boats were needed. A little fleet of yachts, launches and trawlers were all heading out. I was helping launch the boats, sometimes up to my neck in sea, desperately trying to hang on as the boats pitched all over the show and the undertow tried to suck me out. Then someone from the surf club came racing over and said they needed an extra hand on the oars, so off I went on this surf boat, *Miss Europa*. Christ, it was hard work. My arms and shoulders ached for days after.' Frank rubs his arms instinctively.

'I was glad to be out there, though. Much better than just watching, feeling helpless. Don't know how long it took us to get out there, but the sea was still littered with people floating in their lifejackets, like oranges tumbled out into the water. I saw one woman float past with no lifejacket on and water coming out her mouth. She must have been dead. We couldn't stop for those ones; we couldn't even afford to stop for those people we came across who looked all right. We concentrated on the weakest. The ferry crew were great, waving us on to those most in need. We picked up three old men and an old lady whose leg was broken. She was so brave, sitting there with her leg all gone blue, just smiling, rubbing her knee. One of the guys spotted a baby floating by himself in the water, and we thought he was dead – he was totally limp when we lifted him aboard. He lay by my feet and I looked at him several times, I was sure he was dead, but it turned out later he was just unconscious. The waves were still huge, and the boat was drifting all the time out to where the tide going out met the swells coming in. At one point a big wave smashed into us and we almost overturned.

'We passed the ferry which was tipped up on an angle, slowly sinking. We were about to turn back when we saw the black shape of a life raft looming about 100 yards ahead. It looked empty to me, but the guy in charge made us pull on those oars right round it. My arms felt like they would drop off. But there, there we saw two men, grey with cold, clinging to the lines around the raft. We drew up to them and they said nothing, but their eyes – I've never seen such expression in someone's eyes. We hauled them aboard and they lay silent on the bottom of the boat, their grey faces falling against the bright orange of their lifejackets like rotten bits of fruit.

'The breaking seas were dangerously near and we were heading for shore when I turned back and looked up again at the ferry just as it capsized. I could see straight down the funnel before the water poured onto her still hot boiler pipes and a great gush of yellowish steam rushed out. Soon there was only one side of her still above water, slowly going down.'

Frank stops and blinks. His face has loosened, become softer; the skin hangs around his jaw in little folds, a dog-eared book. Martin realises the man is old. One day his own face will look like this, hang in just this way. They both stare through the other. Frank coughs and shuffles, gets to his feet and makes for the stairs. He's halfway up when he calls, 'I'll tell your tape recorder the rest another day.'

Martin looks out the window to the green waves snatching at flickers of afternoon sun as the car winds around the bays. He's not sure what they're doing here, but there's no use asking Frank; he's learnt that much about the man. As soon as Martin arrived today Frank had piled him into the car and driven off without a word. Martin looks across to the older man driving with one hand on the wheel, the other elbow out the window, resting on the car door. His grey hair is riffling in the breeze like the feathers of some old albatross. Martin tries to remember what Frank looked like when he was younger – some of the images from old photos he's seen. The features are the same: the big hawk nose, those steely-blue hooded eyes. The moustache has been there since he was a young man too, but has bushed progressively across his face and changed hue, the salt sprinkles appearing there well before his crop of hair began to grey. The blue bird-eyes flick over at Martin.

'I suppose you're wondering where we're going.'

'Well, yes.'

'You can just bloody well wait till we get there.'

Martin imagines Frank saying the same phrase to a child on a long car journey.

'What's your son doing now?'

'Ian? I've told you, haven't I? He's in Australia.'

'Yeah, but what's he doing there?'

'Being a lazy no-good pot-smoking faggot as far as I know.'

Perhaps this isn't the best time to ask. They pass the Day's Bay pier, and Martin watches a little boy running unsteadily towards the sea – he trips over a sudden log and lands on his face, limbs outstretched in surprise. The mother is there, pulling him upright, before the boy has time to consider translating the anguish on his face into sound. He should ask Connie about Ian.

'So where are we going?'

No reply.

Martin gives up and turns his head back to the sea. It's getting choppy as the wind strengthens. Streaks of white balance on the sea tops and pull together into frothing mouths of foam gnashing down on the rocks. Above, dark clouds slowly knit together, blanketing the sun. Three birds circle lazily over the crashing waves, undisturbed by the tumult below or the ominous darkening above, except when they are occasionally lifted high by a sudden wind. Martin forgets his resolution not to ask Frank anything more until they get to their destination.

'What are those birds?'

Frank leans forward over the wheel and peers up.

'Petrels. Storm petrels.'

At least he answered. Nothing further.

They drive through the village of Eastbourne, with its beach bungalows wedged between tall, architect-designed townhouses colour-washed in Mediterranean orange. Images of old and new New Zealand, in uneasy combination.

Beyond the last of the houses, at the southern end of the village, they pull into a carpark. Martin follows Frank out of the car and looks about him. The hills plunge almost to the edge of the sea, and he can hear the waves thundering down on the shore. He turns to see Frank making his way to a narrow dirt road, and runs to catch up.

'Pencarrow?' he asks.

Frank says nothing, just keeps walking, a long determined stride led by that hawk nose. They walk around Burdan's Gate which spans the narrow gap between the hills and the rocky beach. Martin breathes in salt, feels its grit in his lungs. They stride down the path together like two soldiers intent on following orders. The road bends around a small point, and they parade up to another gate, stout and padlocked, and around either side of it, keeping exact pace with each other. Shortly after, Martin stumbles on a rock and falls behind. He looks out at the bleak coastline stretching southwest, rough pebbly beaches rattling in and out under the strong waves. Occasionally the green water swirls aside to reveal grinning outcrops of rock. Strings of kelp drape over them like jewels on bare necks. They walk and walk.

At last Frank turns, looks out to sea, and speaks. Martin has to come closer to catch the words.

'On April 10 1968, that wasn't so easy. The wind buffeted me all along the motorway and I had to drive around fallen trees and slips all round the coastline. When I finally got out here about 5 pm there seemed to be nothing but dead bodies washed up along here. There were plenty of rescuers by that stage – policemen, doctors and nurses. But it seemed to me they had no one to rescue. I didn't realise until later the survivors had mostly been taken away, either to the hospital or to the RSA in Eastbourne which had been set up as an emergency centre. All I could see were the bodies. Some had no lifejackets on, some hardly any clothes; their skin was blue with cold, their faces frozen in shock, eyes blank, empty.

'It was funny, you know. None of the media had thought to send anyone over here. It was just because I'd been out on that little boat in Seatoun, I'd seen people washing over this way. But nobody knew what was going on out here, nobody knew the conditions. You can't imagine that today, can you? Fucking Paul Holmes would be out here.

'When I got to this point I came across some of the last survivors who had been washed right across the harbour, either on life rafts or simply bobbing along in their lifejackets. There was a young girl helping along an elderly woman, both soaked, clothes ragged, and it was still raining. Their eyes were just as blank as those of the dead bodies. Someone had thrust blankets into my hands as I started out, and I wrapped those around their shoulders, unsure what else to do. A young policeman came rushing up and took the old lady, lumped her over his shoulders like a sack of potatoes, and checked out the girl, asked her if she was okay to walk a bit further where buses were waiting. She said she was, so he told me to keep going, look for people still in the water.

'I kept going, combing the coastline. I met a couple of other guys trying to reach an overturned life raft, so I helped them drag it in – was absolutely soaked by this time myself. We turned it over and slashed open the canopy covering. An old man was stuck underneath, dead. He either suffocated or drowned.'

Frank pauses, his eyes following the rise and fall of the foaming green sea. The clouds are closing in on the two men, eavesdropping. Martin narrows his eyes at them, and tries to imagine this scene more than thirty years ago, that same howling animal from his childhood running loose on the shoreline.

'I tried to get out to some others, wasn't sure if they were alive or not. I swam in, battling the giant waves, until I reached a young woman and dragged her with me back in to shore. But just as my feet could touch the bottom, another monstrous wave roared over, sucked us back out and threw us on the rocks. I lost her, had to let go, and by the time I managed to crawl back into the beach she'd disappeared. There was a little boy, though, I got hold of that little boy all right. I was determined. Bugger the waves, they weren't getting this one. He was so pale, when we got up on shore, so pale, I had to give him mouth-to-mouth until he started breathing on his own. I propped him up with his head on his knees, and he was sick. Someone else was calling for help dragging in a body so I told him to sit tight and went off again. When I got back he'd gone. Someone must have carried him off to the buses. I found out later his father had drowned. I often think of that little boy.'

A long pause, only the sounds of the wind, the sea, the earth heart beating slowly.

'After that there were mostly bodies – poor broken bodies, mainly old people. We gathered them up and loaded them on to trucks and other vehicles. There was one Land Rover about to go which was piled up with about six bodies and I got a hell of a fright when I saw this old woman's hand move. It was terrible. Everybody thought they were all dead. We pulled her out and used the resuscitator on her until she came round.

'I'd had enough by then. There were plenty of people there helping and I had stories to write, though I didn't much feel like it; but I got in the front seat of a truck with this woman and we were taken back to the RSA. We got there about half past six, seven, hardly through the door before we were all being stripped and rubbed down, blankets and soup thrust upon us. They were great, those people. I felt a small measure of the relief the survivors must have been feeling.

'I stayed with the woman whose hand I'd seen move and tried

to look after her, but truth was I was nearly as shocked as her. She was a good old stick, quite cheery really, it was hard to believe we'd just brought her back from the dead. We sat down in a corner with a cup of tea and one of the women from the RSA came over and asked this woman her name. Alma Johns, she said, and the woman said, "Johns? I've just met a Mr Johns over there". We got up and went over to where she'd pointed, and there was this old man wrapped up in grey blankets like a bug in a cocoon. They just looked at each other, these two. "Hello dear," she said. "How are you?" "I'm fine, love," he replied. And they hugged each other.'

Frank stops. He turns away from Martin and strides back the way they've come. Martin looks after him, the old albatross, and his vision blurs. He hasn't seen Frank like this. Cross, stern, yes; he's seen him cheerful and laughing; observed him serious and thoughtful, passionate in espousing some theory or other. But not like this. Touched. That's it. Something has reached into that old bird's heart and squeezed, just gently, to remind him what life is.

An armful of sea crashes at Martin's feet. Drops fly up and sting his eyes. He gasps.

Martin is waiting for Connie. It feels odd being in Frank's house on his own. He wanders about a little, feeling somewhat sinful, keeping his curiosity reined in tight, permitting it to graze over open shelves but refusing it the indulgence of opening and peering into drawers. He wonders if Frank might be back soon. Connie had said he was visiting his nephew. She'd scurried out awfully quickly, almost as soon as he got here. If she didn't want to do this she could have simply said. It's annoying. He's afraid she doesn't like him.

He lets himself saunter down the stairs to Frank's room, pretending not to notice. This may be too tempting. He hopes

Connie will come home soon. The large leather chair sits turned towards him, inviting him to sit, and he does, arms resting on its large buttoned arms, feeling the cracked brown leather like somebody's burnt and peeling skin. He settles back, his head touching the cool material; closes his eyes, imagines he is Frank. The chair even feels like Frank, years of use molding its curves to his, the leather infused with the dark smell of his tobacco. He wonders if the chair is a necessity to the writing, if inspiration comes only when Frank's body is cradled here. His own body feels too small for it, as if he is a boy in a man's chair, and the chair knows it, senses an intruder. Martin opens his eyes and rapidly arises, uncomfortable, his elbows stinging. He blinks and walks around the room until his breathing eases.

Nearly eleven o'clock. He shouldn't have let her go out – all that fuss over tea and biscuits. He didn't need tea and biscuits, she didn't need to go and get anything. He sits down on the other side of the desk, in the hard chair he always sits in, the hard chair for the hard questions. He wonders what he should ask Connie. She's nervous of him, or something – disapproving. Perhaps it is Martin who is nervous of her. He shifts in his seat, looks at the large leather chair and sees the form of Frank, laughing. The old prick. Martin had felt like laughing at him yesterday, but couldn't afford to. He'd been feeling bloody, had sat through a whole morning of Frank's pompous pontifications, adding nothing worthwhile but a few lines to his material, and could not resist saying, just quietly: 'Oh, yes, I talked to Elena Lerner the other day and she mentioned that.'

It was an incredibly delicious moment, just sitting there, watching his face not change. He imagined Frank ringing Elena immediately after he left. Of course then he would find out he had nothing; she would furiously deny. But maybe, just maybe, Frank would be left with a shred of uncertainty, allowing Martin the occasional, brief advantage.

Eleven o'clock. Strange games. After all these months, they still cannot trust each other. Yet some days Frank seems so open, like with the *Wahine* story. Since then things have improved. Martin feels closer to him.

The *Wahine*. A strange gift. He's still not decided quite what to do with it. It sits on his desk at home, unopened. He knows Frank had a purpose in giving it to him. One of his novels had a shipwreck scene – the link is clear there. But that's not all; there's something else. He stands up and goes back over to the other side of the desk, sits in the big brown chair again, slides into it, lets its arms wrap around him. He closes his eyes and lets the question pound against the top of his skull. Martin goes over the story again, the Seatoun drama, but no, somehow the kernel is held at the end, hidden in the straggly bushes near Pencarrow. He hears someone come in the front door and his eyes click open like house shutters. Damn.

He imagines that Connie looks at him suspiciously when he comes into the kitchen.

'I was just downstairs, looking at Frank's bookshelves.'

'Tea then?'

'That would be great.' How can he refuse when she's just walked down to the shops and back for it?

'Go through and sit in the living room.'

Martin sits nervously on the white couch and stares at the expensive Axminster carpet, cream with red roses, green leaves, a similar pattern to the carpet in his grandmother's house when he was young. Maybe that explains this anxiety. What does he know of Connie? What will he ask her? He's seen the way Frank treats her, some aggressiveness there. No wonder she's hostile. She's not, though, not with Frank; she seems to accept him completely, takes whatever he throws at her, as if it's penance. Maybe that's just the generation thing.

'Here we are, dear.'

He doesn't like the 'dear', the falsity. She sets the Royal Albert teapot and cups on the coffee table, pulls it closer to him, goes back to the kitchen for milk and sugar, a small china plate of delicate biscuits. Must eat, must drink, must smile. She sits opposite him, in a straight-backed navy blue chair with winged arms; reminds him of an old school mistress.

'Well this is a change, me being on the receiving end. I see what Frank means now.'

'What does Frank say?'

'He says you're terrifying, the way you cross-examine him. He feels as if he is on trial for something.'

She's making it up. Frank's never been terrified in his life. Rather it is Martin who's fearful, sitting under Connie's beady eye, watching eagerly for the slightest foot out of place, so she can peck him back in.

'Shall we begin?'

He places the delicate cup back on the table with an over-loud chink, and fumbles at his recorder, busies himself with his notebook.

'Tell me about yourself. Whatever you like.'

'Frank has already told you about me, he said.'

'Well yes, a little, but I'd like to know more of your background.'

'I'd rather you didn't put much of me in, if you don't mind, Martin.'

'I don't think you need to worry about that. The book's about Frank. As you're his wife you can see I have to make some mention of you, but that's not really why I want to talk to you. It's more that you can help me understand Frank, how he is as a husband, a father.'

'Are you going to talk to the kids too?'

'I had hoped to, although Frank tells me Nancy's away and Ian's in Australia. Do you know whether he's planning on visiting any time?'

'No, I wouldn't think so.'

Connie is looking down at her hands, strong though mottled

with age, turning her wedding ring round and round a finger.

'Maybe I could write to him. You could give me his address.'

She looks up at Martin narrowly, her eyes like berries stuck into a bun. 'Did you ask Frank about it?'

'Well, no. Not yet. We haven't really got round to it.'

The wedding ring pauses.

'He and Frank don't really get on. Frank doesn't approve of him.'

'Why not?'

'Ian's gay.'

She picks up her china teacup spotted with tiny pink flowers, sips, and sets it down again, passes him the plate of biscuits as if she's made a remark about the weather.

'I was born in Dunedin in 1930. I lived there with my mother until I was twenty-one when I moved to Wellington to be a primary school teacher.'

Martin pulls himself together.

'Your father?'

'He was a Russian seaman, Vladimir Saltykov. I hardly knew him.'

'Yet you have a slight accent, I think.'

The wedding ring begins again.

'My mother was also Russian. She came out to New Zealand after the First World War, as a servant.'

'So you spoke Russian at home?'

'Yes, but mostly when I was very young. My mother wanted me to speak English better than she did. She wanted me to be a New Zealander. And that is what I am.'

'Have you ever been to Russia?'

'Once. But let us talk about Frank. I met Frank at the end of 1954 in Wellington. I was teaching in Karori, and one day we went on a trip to see Parliament. Frank showed us around the Press Gallery – reluctantly, I must say. He didn't like kids much.' She smiles. 'He seemed to like talking to me, though.'

'So you began seeing each other?'

'Yes. We got married at the beginning of 1956 and lived in the Aro Valley, in a tiny little cottage which looks exactly the same today.'

'What was he like then?'

'Frank? Very much the newspaper man. He was writing also, short stories mainly. I think he started *Story of the River Stones* when I was pregnant with Nancy. That would have been 1957–58.'

He listens to her stream of words, watches them flow into his tape recorder, wind themselves around the tiny spinning wheels: names, dates, events, all precisely placed, a careful construction for him to walk around. Except that all the doors are locked. An old lady in a purple cashmere cardigan, with kindly eyes and sugar biscuits, standing stubbornly in his way. The only thing stopping him throwing a tantrum is the sudden clear knowledge that he needs her; she's one of the keys. He tries to explain.

'I need to know more than this, Connie. I need to know what makes Frank tick.'

He tails off, and she smiles at him with a hint of sympathy.

'You have most of what you need before you: Frank himself.'

'No, no . . .' A force grips and climbs his throat, pushing the words down under it. 'I don't know Frank. I need to know him.'

'You will never really know him, Martin. He will not let you.' Her lips seem hard and tight, red lines pulled taut.

He is flailing.

'You know him.'

It could be a question.

'Yes.'

This is useless. He doesn't know what to say, what he wants from her.

'I need your help.'

The plea is direct, honest, personal. There's nothing else he can say.

The blue of her eyes looks tired and worn, like shells rubbed down by countless tides. She sighs softly, settles back a little in her chair.

'What do you want to know?'

'Why don't you tell me?'

Breath indrawn again. Don't piss her off.

'Tell me about Frank as a husband. Tell me about your relationship.'

She turns her head to look out the huge windows, down to the sea swaying there gently like blue-grey maize in the wind.

'We've been happy together. We understand each other, after all these years. Perhaps we didn't really first of all; perhaps we didn't really understand ourselves. We both made mistakes, but we forgave each other.' She looks up at Martin, her lips twitching as if a silent laugh is hovering around her mouth. 'He's a grumpy old b, I know. Sometimes he makes me furious. But I love him. I love the way his mind works.'

'What was he like as a father?'

'The kids would tell you he was hard. But that was what he knew, you see. His father was a hard man. I remember when I first met his father, William – he must have been about sixty-five, already failing. He died five years later. He wouldn't make any concessions to his health, though, treated his body roughly, the way he treated his family. If it didn't perform to his satisfaction, it would be made to perform. He insisted on getting up at the crack of dawn each morning – baker's habits, you see. There was no need any more; would've done him a darn sight better sleeping in those mornings, but no, he was up and dressed, sitting impatiently at the breakfast table at 6am. Old . . .' She pauses and smiles, not at Martin, but vaguely, down at the patterned carpet. 'I guess he was about the same age as I am now.'

She looks up again at Martin; her pupils narrow into focus.

'Would you like some more tea?'

'No, no, no, no. Please, go on. His father?'

'His father. As far as I can tell, that man wouldn't let anyone near him, not even Deirdre. He certainly always pushed Frank well away. Of course by the time I met him, he and Frank had established their adult relationship, they knew exactly where they stood. But I often imagined Frank as a child, reaching out . . . I could see that later, in the image of Ian, reaching out. He adored his father. He wanted to be just like him, you see.'

Martin is unsure if she is talking about Frank or Ian.

'This little boy, looking for someone to follow, someone to model himself on, and only this cold, unloving figure, locked up so securely no one else could ever get in. He must have fought for a long time.'

She is looking right at him now. He fumbles with his glasses, pulse ticking at his temples; wonders if she can see the gleaming in his eyes behind.

'Early betrayals are often repeated later in life,' she says, 'and usually against the people we most love.'

For some reason Martin thinks of Alice.

'What do you mean?' Had Frank betrayed her? Or is she talking about Ian?

'Guilt can be a tremendous thing, Martin, as you may discover. It can be remarkable used creatively. Quite transforming.'

No little old lady here. He looks at her anew. Her thin, pale lips are still tight, but the corners are pulled upwards into a wry, small smile. It expects something from him.

'Do you know guilt?'

'Yes.'

'How? When did you first feel it?'

He is unsure. 'I guess as a child. I remember getting my brother in trouble.'

He doesn't know why he's telling her this.

'Carl was always Dad's favourite, and it used to infuriate me. There was nothing he could do wrong. One day I was in Dad's study – we were never meant to go in there. I was just looking around really, reading the titles on the shelves, picking up paperweights, sitting in his chair, that sort of thing. Suddenly I heard someone coming home, so I jumped down and knocked this precious glass goblet off the desk. It was some sort of prize that my father had won. I was terrified, and without thinking I ran straight up to Mum and Dad as they were coming in the front door and told them Carl had just broken the goblet. The funny thing was, Carl never denied it, never protested. He stood there and took the thrashing. Just looked at me. I felt remarkably pleased at the time; it was only later that night the guilt set in.'

'You know how it feels to do someone wrong then.'

'Yes.'

They sit together quietly a moment.

'Tell me more about Ian, Connie. Is their relationship very strained?'

'They still see each other, every few years. But it was very bad when Ian first came out. He was nineteen or twenty I think. Frank threw him out.'

'What did you think?'

'I thought he was brave. I still do. He knew Frank, he knew what would happen, and yet he stood up for himself. He didn't want a life of lies, living behind secrets. I am proud of him for that, for having the courage to stand up for the truth. Frank will never have that courage. I will never have that courage.'

The tape clicks off. Martin doesn't dare move.

'I will give you two more things. The first thing is: read the books. Read every line, each word, for Frank is there, so clear, so large, that no one sees him. There, floating in the white space, you will see what is Frank, what is not. You may even find the truth.'

She gets up and leaves the room. What? He hears a bird peep outside, as if it has heard his thought: What? What? What? He's confused by all this talk of guilt, and the revelation about Ian. What is he to do with that? He will have to tread carefully with Frank on that one.

When Connie comes back she is carrying a small box. She gives it to Martin and he opens it. Diaries. His eyes widen quickly, close up again.

'Frank has forgotten to give you these,' she says.

He looks up at her, gets to his feet.

'Why?'

She looks disarmed, vulnerable again. Martin, ashamed, lowers his gaze to the box.

'Because I can see you are like Frank. Perhaps you can help him. I no longer can.'

Their eyes meet again, each a little coy.

'Perhaps you can help each other.'

Chapter 5

'There, floating in the white space, you will see **what is Frank,** *what is not.'*

Martin sits at his word processor, yawning, rubbing his eyes. He should have slept longer – his mind is blurred, fuzzy at the edges; he can't concentrate. He stares at the screen, a grey concrete on which has been engraved in small black letters: Chapter 5. He underlines it. How to begin? He looks at his chapter outlines and flicks through the printed pages of chapters one to four sitting neatly on his desk in a blue folder.

There is always more to do. You can always do better.

He sighs and closes the folder, opens it again, rearranges the pages back into their proper order, and sets them aside. Everything seems flat. The material with which he was happy yesterday now seems dull and meandering. There's too much; that's the problem. He looks at the piles of books leaning against his desk like ancient rock formations, the reams of transcripts stacked next to the printer, and fingers his paperweight anxiously, rolling it in his palm like a touchstone.

In 1970 Finnigan made a decision. He would quit his job, move to Nelson and write full-time. His place of birth, Nelson was a small town positioned on a natural harbour with beautiful beaches and bays, and acres of rich, fertile land stretching out to the west, horticultural plains and orchard valleys fortunate to receive the highest annual sunshine reading in the country. But it wasn't an easy move.

Read the books, Connie had said. She's right. That's what counts, the work, not the life. That's what Frank had argued too, long ago, when he had been so vehemently against a biography. Why had he changed his mind? That guy in Hamilton, the one who said he was going to write one anyway: what's happened to him? Maybe he found the task of biography as impossible as Martin does. Can the work and the life be dissociated? No. There are constant parallels. Frank just laughs at him of course. It unnerves Martin, the way he does that. That deep little chuckle that gradually works its way up into a guttural laugh, and twists into an explosive, wheezing splutter. Just when Martin thinks he's found something, that gravelly rasping hacks into his confidence. He shifts in his seat, frowns. His screen saver clicks on and large red words rudely blare across the blackness. *Where do you want to go today?* He sighs, goes to get a cup of coffee.

On his return, he picks up a book from the teetering mountain beside his chair and flicks it open randomly, looking for inspiration. Here's Virginia arguing that biographers and historians are incapable of writing truthful accounts of society: 'for only those who have little need of the truth and no respect for it – the poets and the novelists – can be trusted to do it, for this is one of the cases where the truth does not exist.'

Woolf was well known to be a mad woman. He flicks forward to Kenner.

'Biography is a minor branch of fiction. It's hard to think of a biographer's stratagems that hasn't its antecedent in Walter Scott or Dickens . . . Each biographer has no choice save to flesh out his man from his idea of his man: from what he is capable of imagining. "Creation of character" it used to be called.'

Martin laughs. He very much doubts he is capable of imagining Frank. Here again is the rare advantage of working with a live subject. He will not accept such arguments: it cannot be fiction, because it deals with facts. Such pretensions pose as cover for mere ignorance.

He slams the book shut and sits down before his computer, snaps off the screen saver with a jab at the space bar. He checks his card catalogue, finds the appropriate transcripts, letters and journal numbers, arranges them around his computer like sheaves of an open fan, and reads over what he's written. He deletes it all and starts again.

In 1970 Finnigan made a decision. He would quit his job, move to Nelson and write full-time. It was difficult, as he still had to support his young family, and while his third novel, A Night in November, had just come out to reasonable reviews, his writing was still not earning half of what he made as a journalist. His financial situation was aided considerably by the fact his younger brother Tom had taken a job overseas and had offered Frank the rent-free use of his house. As well as drawing on their small savings for a couple of years, Frank supplemented his income with the occasional editorial for the Nelson Evening Mail.

The leaders make Martin smile, they are so Frank. He leafs quickly through a scrapbook of them and adds a few lines:

The editorials display all the vigour and passion of the man himself. He turned the cannons of his fearsome intellect on a diverse range of subjects from local issues to the Vietnam War.

He wonders if he should include an example, maybe one on the war. He makes a note to himself.

But his real passion he saved for his fiction. He would rise at 6 am and work until noon, producing several thousand words. He would then have a break and do various chores, garden, go fishing, eat dinner with the family, and from 7pm to 10 o'clock he would go over what he had written that day, revising and editing the work, the idea of which had come to him in a dream one day when he lay ill. Little did he know the book, which then had the working title of, simply, A Fable, was destined *to have such an impact and would become an international bestseller.*

Martin pauses. Perhaps he's being overly dramatic. Frank did have some idea of the book's importance, or so he had said. Look at the transcript:

M: But what did you think at the time you were writing it? Did you have any hint it would be as successful as it was?
F: Well, I usually say no. And that's true, in a way, I didn't know it would be as important as it's become. But I did know it was significant. As soon as I read . . . as soon as I looked back over the fully formed manuscript, only then, at that point did I realise. This was something. I really had something. There was nothing else like it.

Something there in what he said. Martin thinks over the conversations he's had with Frank about *The Game of the Few*. It's almost as if he doesn't like talking about the book for some reason; he often seems reluctant, changes the subject, doesn't fully expand the way he normally does. Perhaps Martin is just impatient, because this book is such a magnet for his interest. Maybe it just seems like avoidance. After all, it's a long time ago now, almost thirty years, and Frank must get sick of people always asking about the blockbuster, as if it's the only one he wrote. He needs more, though: something is elusive. The period when Frank was writing it, 1970–71, is covered in those journals Connie gave him. He finds 1970.

The night after Connie had given him the four notebooks, Martin stayed up until 4 am, avidly scouring the spider-scrawled ink blotches for revelations. There was a fairly major one too, if he's got it right – it looks like she had an affair. It's hidden in some odd references to Frank discovering 'Connie's secret activities': I look at her in a new light now. Sometimes I catch myself looking at her, wondering how it could be I could know so little about the woman I loved, the woman I married, the wife who has borne my children. It must be an affair, but there's nothing concrete enough to use. So why did Connie give the diaries to him? Does she want him to ask Frank about it? And how can he, without revealing he's got the journals and how he obtained them?

Martin feels worried by it and vaguely disappointed that the diaries offer nothing he's really looking for – nothing he can seize on as it, the nugget of gold. He wants writing secrets, not tawdry sex. It's as if Connie has let him down, promised him a secret, then failed fully to reveal it. He wonders if she even read the diaries. He hasn't gone back to them since that first fast reading, worry and resentment steering him away, towards other potentially greater rewards. Now he opens up the first one again to March 6, 1970: I haven't been able to write in here for a while.

Martin checks back to the last entry. Date: January 27. Unusual for Frank to go so long without an entry. He flicks back to March.

Last month I made a discovery, which stopped me in my tracks. Two discoveries, in fact. I still can't write about it, but picking up this diary again tonight I have a need to write anyway – to consider, in a way, whether what I'm doing is right.

I feel insulted. I'm fucking offended. I still can't believe it happened, it's so impossible to contemplate. It made me so angry, more bloody angry than I've ever been in my life and I didn't know what to do with it. I couldn't control it. I could've done anything when I first discovered them, and what a way to discover such a perversion! If it hadn't been for Smithson coming in like that with a box of bloody apples for the kids, I could've hit her, hit them both. I never liked the friendship between them from the start. I could tell JS was after something more, but I could scarcely have believed it of Connie. Lying like a flatfish. It's impossible to forgive her.

The anger's mainly gone now, only a thin residue remains, will always remain. But that wasn't the only gift. The other I would never have expected either. Such a fool, a damned blind fool. I'm going to take it. I surely deserve something from her. I've decided that's my due. We've agreed not to speak of it again.

Martin reads the paragraphs over. He feels the same frustration, as he had that first night, combing every page for a breakthrough. It must be an affair: sounds like he walked in on them. A perversion, he calls it. Who is this JS? He will have to go through lists of friends from that period. He hates not being able to take it to Frank to go over, but he can't, not yet. Perhaps he could try asking Connie about it first?

Martin flicks through the pages in frustration: Frank reconsidering Connie, working on the book, the writing routine, the renovations to the house, drinking with journalist buddies from the Mail. The writing stuff is the most interesting, of course.

I worked again on *The Fable* today. It has a glorious, naturally in-built structure to it, I see that now. It all flows so naturally, I dare not disturb it much with my own demands. I'm just sitting back and letting it take me where it will. It's the ride of my life.

The character of Rex Widdens, I have to admit, is my favourite. I try not to play favourites — they can sense when you like one more than the other and turn against you. Still I can't help but admire Rex. He's brave, imaginative, never conscious of his great failings or his inability to achieve any really intimate association. Of course, that's not entirely a problem of his own making. But the way he strives to overcome it is something. I'm not half the man of Rex Widdens.

I'm very happy with the piece I added today, about his first experience of a full-time job. I got the futility and boredom exactly.

Other days he's raging and miserable.

The black mood gripped me again today. I can't believe those nagging bloody voices that cry out my inadequacy. I fucking won't. I've a chance here, the best chance I'm likely to get. It's all so clear, surely a reasonably simple task to shape the thing, but it's not as easy as that. The fucker bucks and turns under my reins and throws me off. I punish the bastard then, bully it into submission – I will make it my own.

Yes, some of this stuff is very useable. Here it comes closest to what he's looking for.

This book is so unlike my others. I'm already itching to have this draft complete so I may go on to the next which, right now, seems to be where all the fun lies. Connie describes it like baking a cake. I've a terrific base to work with, the exact measures of flour, sugar, eggs, milk, and I have to mix carefully. But next, the next stage is the exciting one, where I may choose to add such juicy titbits, the vanilla essence, the currants, the lemon zest. The third draft is the actual baking, where it's vital to ensure an even temperature to enable the whole to cook throughout, rising perfectly. The publication is taking it out of the oven, and the reviews, well, the reviews will no doubt be the cooling-off period. Then my reader gets to eat it up.

I'm already apprehensive about the publicity. As to where the idea came from, where does any idea come from? One minute it's simply there.

No mention of the illness or the dream of which Frank had told him. You would think he would've been sure to note that in his diary. Martin skims through the pages again, but no. He must have been too ill. But here, look: here is a clear premonition.

I am convinced it was the right decision to move here, even with all that's happened since. Writing must be the central purpose and aim of my life. Everything else must be secondary. After such trials, and some errors, I feel on the verge. This, this book will be my breakthrough.

Martin goes back over what he's written, revises it and inserts some of the diary. There, that's made a start anyway: over the hurdle of another thousand words. At some stage he'll have to tell Frank he's using the secret diary. But Frank won't be happy with any mention of the affair. It's not that relevant anyway, simply gossip. Publishers would like it, of course, but they don't have to know. Wait, wait until it's almost done, once Frank fully trusts you, then talk to him.

Alice is knocking at the door of the study. He feels a tic of annoyance.

'Hey, hon, how's it going? I've got you some more coffee.'

'Thanks. Getting there slowly. What do you think of this?'

He skims over it again as Alice reads over his shoulder.

In 1970 Finnigan made a brave decision. He would quit his job, move to Nelson and write full-time. A brave decision, for he still had to support his young family, and while his third novel, A Night in November, had just come out to reasonable reviews, his writing was still not earning much more than half of what he made as a journalist. His financial situation was aided considerably by the fact his younger brother Tom had taken a job in Canada and had offered Frank the rent-free use of his house in Hardy St, Nelson. As well as drawing on their small savings for a couple of years, Connie sold her own knitwear through a shop in town and Frank supplemented this meagre income with the occasional editorial for the Nelson Evening Mail.

The editorials display all the vigour and passion of the man himself, full of fiery sentiments. He turned the cannons of his intellect on a diverse range of subjects, from the most parochial, such as the demolition of the local post office, to global controversies such as the Vietnam War.

(* include eg of editorial)

But his real passion he saved for his fiction. Finnigan didn't know it then, but the solution to his precarious finances lay in the embryo of a manuscript on which he was working each morning. He would rise at 6 am and work until noon, producing several thousand words. He would then have a break and do various chores, and later, from 7 pm to

10 o'clock, he would go over what he had written that day, revising and editing the work, the idea of which had come to him in a dream one day when he lay ill. Little did he know the book was destined to have such an impact on the country of his birth and would become a world bestseller.

Once he had finished the first draft of the manuscript, though, he began to see its potential. 'I didn't know it would be as important as it has become,' he says. 'But I did know it was significant . . . I really had something. There was nothing else like it.'

At the time he described himself in his diary as being 'on the verge', and wrote, somewhat prophetically; 'This book will be my breakthrough.' At that stage the book had the simple working title of A Fable. While at times a 'black mood' would fall on him, most of the time the story simply flowed naturally. He wrote in his journal at the time: 'I'm just sitting back and letting it take me where it will. It's the ride of my life.'

At times Finnigan became impatient to finish and his frustration is apparent in his journals. However, often he also expresses a sheer delight, as in this analogy comparing writing to cooking: 'I have a terrific base to work with, the exact measures of flour, sugar, eggs, milk, and I must be careful not to overbeat. But next, the next stage is the exciting one, where I may choose to add such juicy titbits, the vanilla essence, the currants, the lemon zest. The third draft is the actual baking, where it is vital to ensure an even temperature to enable the whole to cook throughout, rising perfectly. The publication is taking it out of the oven, and the reviews, well, the reviews will no doubt be the cooling-off period. Then my reader gets to eat it up.'

'What do you think?'

Alice murmurs non-committedly.

'You don't like it?'

'No, no, it's fine, Martin. It's fine.'

'But it's not good?'

He feels his shoulders tense up, as if waiting for a blow. It's fine, just go back over it later, spice it up. She doesn't know what to look for.

'It just all seems a bit . . . scanty.'

She has no idea about the process of writing something like this. But why does she always have to be so damned negative?

'It's just a first draft.'

'I know, dear. I'm sure it will be great when it's finished.'

Martin feels like wailing.

'What's wrong with it? Tell me how to fix it.'

Alice perches her bottom up on his desk and Martin suppresses a sudden desire to push her off.

'I'm just not getting much of a feeling for him, you know what I mean? It's fine as it goes, hon, just fine, but you need to engage me more.'

Always so fucking critical. What would she know anyway? She's only a nurse. Martin sighs and clicks his fountain pen on the wooden desktop.

'Readers don't want to wade through an engagement book of dates. I'm not saying this is like that, it isn't. But maybe add some more interpretation, more speculation, more you.'

'But it isn't about me!'

'Well . . . add more of him, then. Just put somebody's spirit into it. It needs something personal. That's what John always says: the personal illuminates the universal.'

John. He hates the way she quotes fucking John. Martin looks resentfully at her, and for a minute it looks as though Alice might even laugh at him. He wills her not to. He couldn't bear it.

'I'm sorry, sweetheart, I don't mean to be dispiriting.'

'Dispiriting? You're downright depressing.'

Alice does laugh and Martin's fingers twitch. Bitch.

'Just relax more, you'll be fine. Find something to bring it to life, look for some force in the stuff. Like . . . here where you mention how he got the idea, can you expand on that? How did he get the idea?'

'He had pneumonia,' Martin replies gloomily.

'What?'

'He had pneumonia and he lay in bed with a fever for four days and he kept falling in and out of sleep and he dreamt the first 100 pages of the story.'

'There you go, use that! Just start right in on that. Forget this introductory bit about moving to Nelson, you can explain that later. Start right in on how he became inspired when he was ill. Readers will love that.'

'Perhaps you could leave now.'

That little laugh again. Alice kisses him and pats him on the head. He resists the urge to pull away.

'Sorry, sweets. Don't mind me. I'll leave you in peace.'

Once he hears the door shut behind her, Martin leans his head on the desk and closes his eyes. He must remember Alice means well. It's just she's been so annoying lately, so critical. He hates that habit of hers of telling everyone just what they have to do, to make things right. She's been doing it even with Lance: she won't let the boy do anything for himself first, must always tell him what to do. What the hell has happened to her lately? Or maybe it's him who's changed. That sense of loss. No, Alice is definitely different. It's that John. Perhaps he should go away for a while, work on the book somewhere else. He doesn't need these interruptions, this pressure.

Martin doodles on a piece of paper. He turns it over to check there's nothing important on the front. It's a list of possible titles. He still can't decide. The title is the first thing readers see, the first impression that contributes to their random judgement to read, or not to read. Most biography titles seem to have something to do with 'A Life', but Martin doesn't like the sound of that. It feels too prescriptive. He reads over the list.

Frank Finnigan, A Life
The Life of Frank Finnigan
The Life and Times of Frank Finnigan
The Life and Opinions of Frank Finnigan
Memories of Frank Finnigan

The road from Nelson: the biography of Frank Finnigan
The story of Frank Finnigan
A biography of Frank Finnigan
The finale: Frank Finnigan's biography

His foot is going to sleep. Martin stumbles up, feeling the blood tingle as it rushes back through the veins. He goes over to the Fs in the bookshelf and looks through Frank's titles, in order of publication. *The Story of the River Stones; Ducks on the Pond; A Night in November; The Game of the Few; To the Homeland;* the short story collection *Plums; When the Wind Blows; The Bones of my Father; And We Awake To The Voices of Angels;* another anthology, *The Stories of Frank Finnigan; Prelude;* and the latest, a slim volume of poetry, *Amusing Elegies.*

He picks up *A Night in November*. He'd meant to check out that shipwreck scene. He flicks through the book, reading a few pages as he walks about the room stamping his foot occasionally.

The winds were whipping up a fearsome storm outside the cabin and Jack could hear men yelling up on deck.

'What's happening Dad?' he asked his father, whose face had darkened like the sky, eyebrows knitting together to form his own personal storm clouds.

'I don't know, son. I'd better go see. You stay put and don't even think about going anywhere until I get back.'

The boy sat on his bunk bed watching the sprays of rain dash themselves against the porthole and swallowed hard. He hoped his father would be back soon. He felt like he might chunder. A sudden gust of wind picked up the boat and there was a loud creak and then a crash up on deck. Jack tried to hold on to his bunk but the cabin tipped up and over, until it seemed almost upside down and Jack was hurled across the room to land with his face pressed flat against the porthole which was now completely covered with green water. Somewhere someone was screaming. The ship righted itself again and Jack slid back across the room to hit his head on the side of the bunk. He was sitting there, rubbing his forehead, when his father flung himself back into the room, frantic.

'Jack! We're going down.'

'What?'

'The ship is sinking, quick, put this lifejacket on, we must go up on deck.'

Up on deck there seemed to be hundreds of people, pushing and shoving, everyone yelling at once, especially when a large wave or wind gust sent them all scurrying for something to cling on to. Jack saw the skipper in a white cap directing the crew to release the lifeboats. His father grabbed him by the hand and dragged him over to the nearest one. But the crew there were holding people back, letting the women board first.

'I've got a child! I've got a child!'

His father yelled against the wind until he was hoarse, then lifted Jack up for the sailor to see. But it was too late, they were crying 'All full' and lowering the swinging lifeboat into the crashing sea below. Someone directed his father over to a lifeboat on the port side where there were fewer people. Halfway across another freak wave whacked the ship's stern, pulling Jack out of his father's grasp and sending him spinning over the deck, smashing into a railing. He felt a hand clutch on to his collar and haul him back on to his feet. The sailor was grinning, a wild, mad leer.

'Nearly lost you there!'

He bundled Jack over to the lifeboat and was lifting him in when his father appeared, holding his elbow, a cut bleeding above his left eye.

'That's my son!'

And he was climbing over the side before anyone could stop him, all thought for his injured elbow forgotten.

'Hey, hey, it's women and children first. Where's his mother?'

'She's not on board, I have to stay to look after him.'

And there was a great creak as the cables began to be lowered and suddenly the lifeboat lurched, practically falling into the boiling ocean. Jack huddled close to his father, who seemed hardly aware he was there, so intent was he on clenching a hand strap. A little trail of blood spattered his face from the cut above his eye, like the erratic path of a raindrop down a window pane. A woman lay in the bottom of the boat, moaning that she had broken her leg, but no one paid her any mind; someone was even sitting on her other leg. About fifty people were piled into the tiny boat which was being thrown up and caught again by the sea. Jack was sick, a little stream of bile that dripped down his orange lifejacket. He pulled at his father's arm but the man looked straight through him.

All at once a great wave came up under the boat and tossed it up into the air. There was a scream, as if from the boat itself, and Jack found himself plunged into the icy green tide, washed back and forth like a scrap of seaweed. The salt slapped his face and made him cough. He noticed the water had washed his bile away. There was a man floating not far away and Jack tried to paddle his way towards him. More by chance than design, the two were flung together by the waves and Jack gripped on to a strap hanging from the man's lifejacket.

'Dad!'

It was his father, gasping and retching like a drunk.

'Dad!'

The man shook his head and looked at him through red-rimmed eyes.

'Jack. Thank God.'

He clutched at him until Jack felt queasy again and shook him off a little. The boy could see a few other spots of orange in the distance, people floating away in the waves, helpless. To the right was a large shape, perhaps a piece of the lifeboat, which had vanished. Jack pointed at it and urged his father to swim with him towards it. It seemed to take an age, dog-paddling uselessly towards the debris, only to be washed back again by the rolling sea. Eventually they stopped kicking and almost immediately found themselves next to the piece of wood. His father perked up a bit, his pale face briefly alert again as he reached towards it. The man weakly clambered up on to the object and looked about him.

'Dad!'

It was as if his father had only just remembered he was there. He put a feeble arm out towards Jack, but couldn't reach.

Jack pushed himself towards the wood and managed to get a handhold, and heaved himself up, but the object rocked precariously and his father cried out.

'No Jack. There's only room for one.'

'Dad!'

'You just hold on there, and keep kicking. You'll be fine. You're young.'

Jack held on and leant his head against the side of the slippery wood. It was cold and he couldn't stop shivering. The waves were swelling with the tide. It felt as if they were being drawn steadily towards something.

'What can you see, Dad?'

There was no answer.

'Dad, Dad. What can you see?'

He gripped his father's foot and the man looked down at him. He looked as grey as the sky.

'Jack.'

A large wave scooped them up and dashed them down again, and the man looked back out to sea.

'What can you see, Dad?'

'I can see the shore, son. We're heading towards land.'

They said no more after that. Jack concentrated on clinging to the wood, counting the swells under his breath. The waves were gathering force, building up so his counting became slower and more difficult. Jack thought he could hear a wild crashing in the distance. They must be close to shore. He looked up at his father, whose head had slumped forward so that his chin rested on his lifejacket. His hands seemed limp.

To begin with, it felt as if someone was gently lifting him from behind, reluctant to wake him, and then he was shaken violently and plunged under salty green sea until his ears began to ring and he felt himself slipping into blackness, before he was pulled up to the surface again and slapped conscious by the waves. He had lost his grip on the wood. Neither it nor his father was anywhere to be seen. Jack had no time to look further or call out. The sea had him by the scruff of his neck, and was bullying him forwards. The undertow sucked at his feet and only his lifejacket resisted, then it let go and they spiralled backwards, under torrents of water, and he was thrown high again, landing hard, his breath thumped out of him, sprawled on the rocks. He lay there a while, nudged forwards by the sea, its spray licking at his white white face.

He must have managed to crawl up on to the shore somehow, for he found himself later curled on soft sand, his scratched and battered arms flung about him. He couldn't remember how he got there. Jack lay and listened to himself breathing. He was alive. After a while he gingerly stretched his aching limbs and sat up. The wind had quieted and the sea was lapping softly at the rocks now. There was no sign of any other life, save a sole, lonely bird wheeling in the grey sky above. Jack knew his father was dead, yet he felt nothing. It was as if his father had died a long time ago and he was just remembering the fact.

What is it Connie said about Frank's parents? They're important somehow. Perhaps this can be brought into the analysis of the writing. There are certainly plenty of instances of an underlying guilt syndrome. Perhaps the father – yes, the father, the remote, rejected father. That fits. Yes, easily carried over into impulse of parricide, son's guilt over murderous wishes. He must look more closely at what Frank has said about the father–son relationship in his writing. Here, here is an explicit case. What has he said about *A Night in November*?

Martin is ferreting through his files and doesn't notice the door open and someone come in until Lance is standing behind his chair.

'Hi, Dad.'

'Hi, hi.'

He hasn't started a separate filing system yet for each title – he must do that, it really is much too muddled like this, he can't find anything. Didn't Frank describe *A Night in November* as his most exciting novel somewhere? Now where was that?

'Can you come and help me with a maths problem, Dad?'

'What's that? Maths? Your mother will help you. She was always better at maths than I was.'

'She said to ask you.'

It was in one of those early conversations about the impulse to write. He really should label these transcripts better.

'Dad, Mum said you would help me.'

'Can't you see I'm busy, Lance? I haven't got time. Go tell your mother I'm too busy and she'll help you.'

So many bloody interruptions. He should go away somewhere. Martin stands and looks up at Lance, exasperated. A page works its way out from the midst of the pile of transcripts in his hands, and floats to the floor like a large white feather. The boy is growing. Only eight and his eyes are nearly level with Martin's chest. Martin has an urge to put out a hand and stroke him on the cheek. But he's glaring.

'Bloody, bloody, bloody!'

The door slams and the boy is gone.

'Language!'

Martin feels shock pricking under his eyelids, itching. He turns back to the desk and blinks, picks up the single white sheet surrendered on the floor, and turns it over absently:

F: It's an escape I suppose.

That's it. That's the section. Martin finds the consecutive pages and sits at his chair, excited.

F: It's an escape I suppose. That's one reason. You get to go somewhere else, anywhere you want. You get to be anyone you want to be. I've had so many different lives I've lost count.

M: A good enough reason. So do you feel as if you are living the life of each character?

F: No, no. (Coughs) No, it's not like that, that's going too far. Although some characters I'm good mates with, I wouldn't say any of them are me, or that I'm living their lives as I write them, no. It's more . . . (pause) it's more like each book I write is a separate journey, another life, if you like. I'm not putting it very well, I'm not feeling so great today. This bloody (cough) cough.

M: That's okay. It's interesting. So, if you've written nine books . . .

F: 12.

M: I wasn't counting the short stories or poetry.

F: I've written 12 bloody books.

M: All right, so you've written 12 books, that's 12 different lives.

F: There's still one damned life going on in front of your eyes.

M: Okay, okay. Tell me, which was your favourite?

(Pause)

Martin remembers what the silence felt like. Heavy and slow, like a cloud welling with rain. Thoughts passed over Frank's face like shadows.

F: My favourite . . . Aah

And the balladeer was back.

F: That would have to be my first, <u>The Story of the River Stones</u>.

Martin had tried not to show his surprise.

M: Why's that?

F: It was my first. I had no idea what I was doing and I was more free than I've ever been since.

M: What was your best book?

F: I suppose if you're judging that by success, it would have to be <u>The Game of the Few</u>. (Quiet, almost whispering) No, that was the best writing too, better than any of my other books.

M: What was your most exciting book?

F: Exciting? Hah. I'll tell you, the third, <u>A Night in November</u>, you remember, the story of little Jack Danby. I wrote that so quickly, it simply poured out in this rollicking great ride, I was breathless with excitement. And you know, I think that shows through eh. Well, readers tell me anyway. Don't you think? People tell me it's exciting to read, the pace of the thing, I guess. I wrote it fast and it sure bloody reads fast, people tell me they can hear their hearts beating reading it, they stay up reading in bed, past their normal lights off, just devouring it.

M: Yes, I know. That was exactly what I did, the first time.

F: You know then.

M: What was your most . . . interesting book, do you think?

F: Interesting. That's a funny word. Well, I reckon maybe the <u>Voices of Angels</u> – <u>And We Awake To The Voices of Angels</u>. I always found the ideas in that novel most intriguing – the interventionist God and so on. I think that one is the most interesting in that way. (Pauses again, stares into distance)

M: What about your own life? How would you rate your real life against all these books as lives? What about Frank Finnigan?

Martin had thought for a minute there he'd lost him. He remembers cringing at his own words circling in the air between them.

F: Frank Finnigan. That life never seemed as true somehow.

At that he got up and went to get a beer. Martin laughs at the remembered image. Old Frank. There's just something about him he loves. He picks up his fountain pen and draws his lips across the metallic top. He starts to type again.

It's quarter to 12 when Martin looks up at the clock. He's been engrossed in his argument; the writing, for once, has been flowing. He feels light-headed, as if thoughts have simply been passing through him and out on to paper. Is this what Frank feels like? Is this a kind of suspension of consciousness?

He looks at what he's written, the list of titles, the comparisons with phases of Frank's life. Frank had described each book as a life. And yet, his own life seemed unreal to him. He types, then pauses: no, Frank had said *untrue*. Martin looks back at the quote in the transcript. That life never seemed as true. Martin slowly types the quote, pauses after the final word, then absently backspaces over each letter: e; u; r; t. He types over r; e; a; l. That sounds better. That life never seemed as real. If Frank's life wasn't real, or true, what was? What was truth? What was reality? Would his biography be any more true than any others? Just another life. The thirteenth life of Frank Finnigan.

Martin yells.

'That's it!'

He must tell Alice. He shoves his chair back and quickly saves his work, shuts down the computer and rushes to find her.

Chapter 6

'It's like trying to explain colour to someone who's colour blind.'

They're back in Frank's study. Although mid-morning, it's gloomy outside and the heavy clouds are following up on their promise of rain. Specks of water spatter the windows. Martin shifts in the hard chair. Frank seems quiet, and Martin is unsure of his mood. He checks the tape recorder once more.

'Get on with it. I'm getting old.'

So, he's grumpy.

Martin eyes Frank carefully. He is getting old – looking older anyhow. Perhaps there are more lines around his eyes, his neck skin is hanging more loosely. He doesn't look very well.

'Perhaps you could talk a little about your sense of humour.'

'You don't analyse humour, Martin. That destroys the point.'

'No, no, I mean in relation to your fiction. Many critics speak about this. They describe your work as being infused with humour.'

Frank yawns. Martin waits until he's finished, then flips over a page in his notebook and places the point of his pen above the paper. Frank sighs.

'Humour. Yeah, well, that's not necessarily deliberate, you know. It just happens. It often surprises me actually, that people find it funny.'

Martin's dumbfounded. 'But surely you must do it deliberately. It's one of your trademarks.'

'Oh well, yeah. I mean I've always had a brilliant sense of

humour, I suppose. I enjoy being sarcastic. You may have noticed. I like observing the irony in the world.'

'So your writing's designed to . . .'

But Frank interrupts, suddenly vehement. 'I've not written one book which I intended to be funny. It's just something I use to support the whole thing. You can't simplify it like that.'

'Oh.' And, 'I see.'

Time to move away from humour.

'You've also written some very moving scenes, like in *Prelude* when Billy returns to his family.'

'Oh, sure. But I knew what I wanted to do, see.'

'So it's deliberate then, you're manipulating the reader?'

No reply. It's one of those mornings.

'Like in *The Bones of My Father*. The scene with Robert and Brian talking sentimentally about their childhoods is followed within a few pages by that outrageous scene at the family get-together.'

'Yeah. I guess that was fairly quick.'

'And the humour heightened the writing.'

Got you.

'Yeah. You see that's what I sometimes do, I use humour as a contrast. Life's not simple, see. And people sure aren't simple. They're not all good or all bad, they're messy. That's what I'm after. For instance, in *The Game of the Few*, Rex may be obnoxious, but in the end you see he has got a conscience after all.'

'Let's talk about *The Game of the Few*. I know you're often asked to compare it to your other books. But if we use the metaphor of your works as children, *The Game of the Few* was what might be considered a genius child and that must have put a lot of pressure on the others.'

'Now there you see that bloody great myth again, about how *The Game of the Few* was the only book of mine that was any good.'

'I didn't say that.'

Shit.

'You bloody better not say that. You've read my books, you've

133

seen my progress. Just because *Game of the Few* was a fucking bestseller doesn't mean the rest were crap. My most recent books are much better. Just look at *Prelude*, the writing in that. Fucking public wouldn't know good writing if it shit on them. And the critics, most of them have the brains of a sheep!'

Here we go.

'All right, Frank, all right. I'm not arguing with you.'

'It's not as if good writing is something anyone can do, you know. It's not like it's just a job.'

'I know, Frank. Let's talk about the process a bit more, shall we? Tell me about your writing schedule again, the way you work.'

Frank is fussing irascibly for his pipe. He finds one in a drawer, and fills it, muttering. Martin pauses the tape until he's settled.

'Right, tell me how you work.'

'I get up, I write, I go to bed.'

'Frank.'

'I get up at 7 am, I fart, have breakfast, take a crap, brush my teeth, come down here and work from 8.30 am till noon. Most days. Sometimes I go on to five, six. Other days I don't start till then and go right through the middle of the night.'

'Frank.'

'But generally I'm a morning man. That's what you want to know, isn't it. Write in the mornings, an average thousand words a day. On my word processor.'

'You don't use a pen sometimes? Or an old typewriter?'

'Are you kidding? These things are brilliant.' He taps the computer. 'Can't understand people who're afraid of them. My old mates on the newspapers, they're always grumbling about new-fangled technology, how it's taking over the world, will make us all redundant some day. Pack of Luddites. Most of them can only type with two fingers – that's what will make them redundant. They need to catch on like the young people, master the machines. This, you see, this is the latest. It can do anything you want it to: print pictures in colour, give you 128 different fonts, tell you what you have to do every day with its electronic diary, play chess with you, whatever you like.'

He's turning it on.

'I know what they look like, Frank.'

'I'll just show you this. I got it the other day.'

He's pressing the key but nothing's happening. He tries another, then another, jabbing his finger as if he's killing an insect, swearing. Finally, a robotic WELCOME FRANK blares from the computer's speakers.

'Hear that? Now, listen to this. I'll just shut it down.'

This time he only has to press twice. Martin hears the final strains of *My Way*.

'Brilliant, eh? I reckon she's a little boomer.'

It's cheered him up anyway.

'Tell me about your planning. Some writers do hardly any, it seems. What's your approach?'

'Ah.' The great pontificator. He clears his throat, coughs a little. 'I don't hold any store in that "no planning" line. See, those writers, they don't really know what they're doing, or if they do, they're lying about it. All writers plan, to a certain degree. Even if they don't have anything written down, they'll have spent a long time brooding on it, walking around the idea, rolling it round in their heads. That's just planning in a different format. I used to do it that way. Nowadays I tend to write most of it down, so I don't forget it.'

The rain claps on the window in applause.

'Have you ever started a book when you didn't know the ending?'

'No – well, yes. It's difficult to explain. I always know what happens, but sometimes in the writing things change. Characters do things you didn't initially envisage, or new characters appear and change the direction. Sometimes I write the endings first. My next book, the one I've just started, I began that by writing the ending first. I'm afraid I won't be able to finish it otherwise!'

He coughs out a laugh.

'What about *The Game of the Few*? Did you know that ending?'

'Um. Yes. Yes, I knew all of that story right from the start.'

'So how did you plan it?'

Frank pauses and turns to watch the rain rattling against the windows in miniature waterfalls.

'I can't remember very well. It was so long ago. I think it was one of those ones I worked out in my head first.'

'So you wait for inspiration.'

Frank gets up from the chair and walks around the room, puffing on his beloved pipe. Martin gulps in the sweet smoke like oxygen.

'No, no, that's a load of bollocks, that New Agey spirituality stuff. You can't wait for "inspiration", whatever the hell that is. That's as much use as a one-armed paperhanger scratching his balls. You just sit down and write. It's a job, like any other. You just get on with it.' He huffs. 'You just write, and then the reviewers tell you what you meant.'

'I thought you didn't read reviews.'

'I don't.'

Frank turns from the window, and Martin sees a beautiful thin rainbow struggling to balance on his head.

'I don't have to read them. I know when it's good or bad.'

Martin tries not to laugh at the unlikely angelic halo of colours. He looks down at his notes.

'So you would subscribe to the author being in complete control.'

'That's right.' He's pacing again. 'You know where you're going and it's just a question of getting there.'

'But you said you're sometimes surprised.'

'Well, yes, sometimes something happens . . . you know, you think of things along the way. It's not that you're not in control, it's just . . . you know, how you revise things. It's just a matter of constantly improving as you work.'

'But . . .'

'Here's an analogy for you. It's like driving at night. You can only see as far as the headlights, but you know where you're going and you can make it the whole way.'

'Do you always know when you've arrived?'

'Well, sometimes you don't. You might stop too early, or even too late. But you find that out in later drafts, when you're refining it. You can see the structure a lot more clearly and you know what has to happen. Mind you, you could go on forever if you let yourself. That's the problem with some writers – that Cash guy, for instance, he goes way over, in my opinion. But it's like painting: you put on layers of colour and then layers on them, and at some point you have to stop and frame it.'

'Did you ever get writer's block?'

'Oh, well, yes. God turns the tap on and off. I suppose there were times. Connie would tell you there were.' He stops and eyes Martin for a moment. 'Early on, especially. I was writing in the dark, you know, unsure of it. I sold okay, but there wasn't that real confidence until after *Game of the Few* made it. I had a long block just after my first book was published, around the time of my father's death. They're hard to cope with. You really believe you'll never be able to write again. I haven't had any for a while now, though. I've relaxed a lot more. I know what I'm doing, who I am.'

Martin recognises a jealousy within himself.

'So you've mellowed with age?'

'Yeah, but I'm not happy about it.' Frank roars with laughter. That distinctive, throaty bellow.

'Have you seen this article in *Landfall* that's just come out?'

Martin scrabbles in the bag at his feet.

'Yes, yes. Don't bother to show it to me again, boy.'

'Well what did you think?'

'Academic twaddle.' But his eyes are twinkling under their bushy camouflage.

'I thought the references to you were interesting.'

'I didn't.'

Martin can't help laughing.

'And that stuff about Tarl Prackett, that's just bullshit. People don't write books to benefit humanity. Writers are simply exhibitionists.'

'Is it nothing to do with creativity?'

'Creativity? Writing's a creative way of getting attention maybe, getting respect.'

'I thought the article made some interesting points. It was intriguing, her speculation that authors could not let their characters do emotionally what they could not do themselves.'

'Fucking crap.'

'You needn't worry, Frank. I'm not going to get into that psychological stuff. I know you don't like it.'

'Say what you think, Martin. I've heard it all before, from better people than you.'

Prick. Here goes then.

'Well I should tell you I believe there are some parallels between the themes of your books and your actual life. I don't need to elaborate. I'm sure you're as aware of them as anyone.'

'You've been reading too many pop-psychology books. You should get yourself a shrink.'

Martin can't bear the contempt.

'The theme of guilt is especially overriding in your fiction. Tell me, Frank, what do you feel so guilty about?'

A flash of a look Martin cannot recognise, followed by Frank's act of general amused superiority. He throws back his head and guffaws. Martin hears Connie on the stairs.

'You men are having a good time anyway. I brought you some tea and sandwiches, since it seemed you were never coming up for them.'

'Great, it's about time we had a break. Put them there, Con.'

Connie is lingering. Martin gets up to go to the toilet. When he gets back Frank is standing alone at the french doors, now open. Martin joins him, and they eat together for a while, silently, looking out at the wet garden and the sea, and Martin feels an unusual camaraderie. The rain has stopped and the world smells fresh and new.

'You know you were talking about writer's block? Just quietly, I've been feeling a bit that way lately. Can't seem to do anything about it. Might be my health, I reckon. I've been feeling a bit crook the past few weeks.'

Martin is unsure what to say. It sounds as if Frank has just admitted to killing someone.

'Talking about writing, like we are today, makes me want it. I miss it, you know, those times when you're just going at it, words coming out and down on the page before you've even realised them fully. That's the writer's highway, Marty. When all the blocks are gone and you're free to go, as fast as you like, no other cars on the road, just go for it. Nothing like it.'

Martin wishes the tape recorder was still on. But this is too good not to pursue.

'So that's the main satisfaction? That's why you write?'

'God, yes. That's it. It's not the success, the praise. It's not even the publication. Well, those are all reasons too. But the drive, the act itself: you can't tell people unless they know it. It's like someone else working through you when it happens. A god.'

Frank sits heavily on the carpet, legs out the door. He pauses, looks up at Martin.

'It's like trying to explain colour to someone who's colour-blind.'

Martin can't stand it any more. He nabs the tape recorder from the desk and brings it over to Frank, switches it on.

'Can you just say that thing again, you know the bit about . . .'

'For fuck's sake.' Frank rises to his feet, pushing the recorder out of his face. 'You just don't get it, Martin. You'll never get it.'

He turns angrily and stomps up the stairs. His words echo down the stairwell.

'You have but two subjects: yourself and me. I am sick of both!'

The words seem vaguely familiar.

It begins raining again as Martin's packing up. He should ring Alice and change the arrangement for him to drop the car at the hospital, but Connie's fluttering around him. She seems to want to talk to him about something, but Frank's in the background. He still hasn't had a chance to ask her privately about JS, but the fluttering's making him nervous. He gathers his things, says a quick goodbye and hurries out to the car.

Martin drives to the hospital in Newtown. He parks and puts on his coat, walks around to the taxi rank – empty. Too impatient to wait, he begins to walk on to the next one. The rain eases off once he gets to the Basin and he starts to think he might walk all the way home. It's a distance, but he's enjoying the exercise. It's been too long since he had a good walk. It helps clear his head.

Frank's funny. Sometimes Martin thinks he's got him all worked out; then he goes and does something, says something, totally contradictory. He still can't get a grasp on what Frank says about writing. One moment it's a special thing, and he's in the grip of some kind of a god, the next moment it's just a job, a completely rational process. In a way, Martin likes the idea of it involving something spiritual, the unconscious; but he needs to believe Frank knows what he's doing. Otherwise it all falls apart. How can he believe in the Author, if the author doesn't?

The wind is getting up. It throws handfuls of light rain against his face, slaps his raincoat around his legs as he walks down Tory Street. He must work it out. He'll have to sit down at home and separate all the strands, follow them to the real heart. It must all come back to the author either way, conscious or unconscious. He must find the meaning, Frank's truth.

Frank. Martin smiles, turns into Courtenay Place, walks past empty tables on the pavement. He shakes himself under the shop awnings, like a dog. Frank's a hard case. In more ways than one. Interesting, his reaction to the subject of humour. Touched a nerve, it seems. That black humour which comes through as a put on in his books, it's hard to separate from the reality. In his books it allows the reader to pierce to the heart. In person, it holds you off.

It's like Rex Widdens, the main character of *The Game of the Few*. He remembers describing Frank that way to Alice once. He must pursue that line more, make more explicit comparisons. He can't remember much of the physicality of Rex, but imagines him rather like a younger Frank. Like Frank in personality too, charming and funny, then restless, sarcastic, cruel. Surely he couldn't have based him on himself so accurately, complete with flaws? It's like someone else looking at Frank.

Alice didn't like Rex. What had she said? Too arrogant, or something. Yeah, Frank was arrogant. It didn't stop you liking him, though; just made him more human. That's the trouble with Alice. She doesn't like humanity much. She'd rather you were perfect, didn't worry about anything, faced the world 'like a man'. What does that mean? She probably means like John: all men should be strong like John. But what about the shadow side of being a man; the doubt, the fear? It has been gnawing at him a long time now. The biography has helped, has come to fill some of that gap, but still that sense of loss, growing keener every time Frank talks of writing. He isn't colour-blind at all. He wishes he was.

A car hoots at Martin as he wanders absentmindedly across Dixon Street. He waves, notices the rain has stopped. His reflection in a shop window makes him pause, and someone nearly bumps into him, mutters. He continues walking, watching the man in the window walk along parallel to him. The man looks older than him; his hair is greying, his face tired and leathery. He looks sad. Martin looks away, walks on.

Striding up the Dixon Street hill, he peers up at St John's. The spire is straight and true. He can hear his breath drawing in and out of his chest. A quote from Dante's Divine Comedy rises in his mind.

> *Midway upon the journey of our life*
> *I found myself within a forest dark*
> *For the straightforward pathway had been lost.*

Perhaps he will just go in and sit a while.

Martin raises his eyes from the book and looks over at Alice, lying beside him in bed. Sleeping at last. Her face is pale and her eyes are flickering under her eyelids. What's she dreaming?

He shouldn't have argued with her. It seems to have become a nightly ritual. Still, she could've stayed home with him tonight. He wasn't working: she didn't need to go out with John and Helen. He wonders if she can feel the resentment as he looks at her, whether it seeps into her dreams. It's been getting worse. One of them is going to snap soon. Martin sighs, lifts the covers and swings his legs to the floor; slowly pulls himself upright. He looks back at Alice, watches her chest gently rise and fall, and picks up his book.

In his study he feels calmer, more at home. He settles into his chair and pokes his feet up under his bum, like a little kid, and picks up *The Game of the Few* again, trying to find the first description of Rex.

Rex stood up to shake her hand and she noticed how tall he was, in a lanky sort of way, his limbs all slightly too long in relation to his body, so he appeared stretched. They sat down, she ordered a drink and looked him over. His short dark brown hair had that flat wave to it that suggested curly hair oppressed and shorn flat; his moustache, a lighter blondy-brown, regulation, neatly clipped. He could be a policeman, or a soldier, but few people would guess what he really was. He was dressed anonymously, camouflaged in an everyday nondescript suit. She felt that he was looking her over too. His grey eyes glittered. He offered her a cigarette.

It doesn't sound much like Frank – well, maybe with his hair and moustache coloured and cut short, before he grew a pot belly, if you took him out of his cardy and corduroys and wedged him into a suit. Why did he think of Rex as Frank, then, and vice versa? He flicks forwards, scouring the pages for clues.

His laugh was loud and guttural, with an edge to it. It warned her not to come any closer. Katherine wondered what had happened to make him so expert at blocking. Perfect for the job, of course, but personally she found it unnerving. How could one form a real relationship with someone so cut off? There must be some way under. No one could have armour that thick. She must look for the chinks, his vulnerabilities.

There, there's a hint of Frank: the blocked emotions. An odd contrast with his writing, or some of his writing at any rate. His characters are often contemptible but given to moments of painful lucidity. Frank, therefore, must have the same capability. He just doesn't like to expose it. To be able to write about it, though, that must be a release. Can he let his characters do what he cannot?

Of course, there is that one article that concludes Rex is a device for the main purpose of the book, the demonstration of the futility of the Cold War. The plot shows it up on a large scale, while Rex demonstrates it on a personal level. The academic goes even further, into issues of national identification, and makes much of the fact that Rex was going to return from England to live in New Zealand; but Martin thinks the bow too long. He's looking for the more personal still, the direct links to Frank, why the guilt portrayed is so successful, so real. This is the first of his books to feature the themes that come to characterise his writing: secrets, deception, lies and guilt. Martin is convinced there is some personal explanation. He recognises the same curiosity he felt on reading *The Game of the Few* for the very first time, but this time he's far less likely to be satisfied.

Martin turns to the final revelation of the book, where Rex's daughter Anna discovers the letter.

Anna waited until the man left the room, then went to sit in one of the large chairs in the bay window. The sun was streaming in and the rose-coloured fabric was warm. She nestled into the cushions like a little girl and looked down at the envelope in her hands. The writing was her father's, the blue ink from his favourite fountain pen. She would not cry, Rex would not have wanted it. She closed her eyes and remembered the last time she saw him. It was at the train station: she could still smell the engine, hear the bustle of people around him. Rex had looked old for the first time. Perhaps he knew, even then; perhaps he anticipated what would happen. He had taken off his hat, to kiss her, and she had clutched at it, wouldn't let it go. He had laughed at her, shaken her off. He was always shaking her off. Now he had really succeeded.

She opened her eyes and read her name again. It was like a nudge. She lifted the edge of the envelope with a fingernail and carefully tore along the edge. The paper within was thin and fragile, the voice of the dead. Anna unfolded the letter and read.

My dearest Anna,

I told you once what I did for a living, and you will have found out by now that I was in fact working for both sides. Don't judge me. You will never know the full reasons. And don't believe what others say about me. I go to my grave with a clear conscience. On that count at any rate. To achieve a completely clear conscience I must write this letter. There is one more thing I must confess, and I can do so only to you. You, my darling daughter, must know who your father truly was.

You know my history in part only. You have heard the tale of how my mother, stepfather and my younger brother Henry all died in a car crash in Australia many years ago, and how I escaped. The facts were not quite as related. Let me tell you now what really happened.

Elsa, my mother, was driving, and beside her in the front passenger seat was her second husband Brian. I was in the back seat with my half-brother. The road around the hill was steep and windy and when that driver, mad or drunk, came at us, my mother had to swerve wildly to avoid him. We crashed through a fence, bumped off rocks most of the way down and ended up, as you have been told, precariously balanced on a precipice over the river. I managed somehow to get out of my side of the car. I cannot remember how. I told everyone afterwards that the others were already dead, or knocked unconscious, and I had no chance to save them. Certainly there was no sign of movement from either Elsa or Brian. But my brother, Rex, was certainly still alive. Yes, Rex. The car took a long time to topple; it swayed back and forth like the slow beating wing of a bird. I stood there and watched. My door was wide open and I could see my brother stretched along the back seat, a trickle of blood at his temple. His eyes were pleading with me and a strange gurgle came from his throat. Rex was asking me to help him, and I just stood there, waiting, and waiting, until at last there was a great creak and the car fell like a tree, spiralling down into the river.

It was after I heard they had recovered the bodies and I had to go to identify them that I decided. I hadn't said much to anyone at that point, which they'd put down to shock. It all came together so easily. We were on holiday in Australia so no one knew us, and there were no direct relatives back in New Zealand. I said I was Rex and that my blood father, James Widdens, lived in Britain. Sure enough they sent me here, and James never knew the difference, having only seen Rex as a baby.

That is my secret. I have been living someone else's life. But what a life, eh Anna? What a life. I only hope yours will be as exhilarating.

With all my love
Your father
Henry Jamieson

Martin closes the book and looks at his watch. Past two. He should go back to bed. He leaves the book on his desk, gathers his dressing gown around him, and shuffles back to the bedroom. Alice has turned over, away from the lamp that still shines at his side of the bed. Martin quietly slides in next to her and turns off the light. He lies in the dark, thinking.

Martin is dreaming. He's driving at night. The road rises up before him like an animal rearing. It is completely smooth and straight. There's no moon, no stars; all is black but for the twin yellow funnels of light from his headlamps. He hears voices behind him. Martin turns around and there in the back seat sit a teenage Frank and a young Rex. They are bickering.

'Put on your seatbelts,' he orders them.

Martin turns back to the road and notices Connie sitting in the front seat next to him. She smiles at him.

'Do as your father says,' she tells the boys.

Martin can hear a large truck coming up behind them. It mustn't have its lights on, for he can see nothing; but there is definitely something there, he can hear it rumbling, louder and louder. He speeds up. Still the truck rumbles on – it is catching them, must be tailgating him. Martin can feel himself sweating. He puts his foot down on the floor and boots the car past 140, over 160, until the needle wavers nervously around 200. Connie is yelling something angrily. Too late, Martin sees the bend in the road, stomps on the brake pedal. The truck is gone, the road is gone, there is nothing but a falling.

'Fuck him!'

Martin crashes down the receiver.

'Martin! What's wrong?'

Alice is going past with an armful of laundry.

'The prick just cancelled.'

Alice grins at him. Bitch.

'Said he "couldn't be bothered". How the fuck does he expect me to finish in time if he keeps putting me off?'

'Your language has definitely deteriorated since you've known that man. You can come with me and Lance to my mother's then.'

So that's why she's grinning. Bugger. No getting out of it now.

'Um . . . yeah, okay. I'll just go tidy up some stuff in the study. Let me know when you're ready to go.'

Martin goes into the study and closes the door behind him. His haven. He would rather just lock himself up in here all day, get some real work done for a change. Why won't she understand that this is important? If only they would just leave him to it. He has to prepare for the interview with Alex MacLeod, type up the last transcript, finish off that bloody chapter six. He looks at it sitting on his desk with that note he's scrawled on top of the first page – finish by Friday!

Trouble is, he has no idea how to finish. He's finding the chapter on *The Game of the Few* much harder than he expected. He doesn't have nearly as much material as he thought, and the focus seems weak. He hasn't organised it right or something. It's lacking point, structure. Every time he looks through the interviews with Frank, he comes up with great gaps and inconsistencies. Each time they start to talk about the blockbuster, Frank somehow turns the conversation away.

No one else is much help on the subject either. Most of Frank's literary friends became so after the bestseller, and his non-literary friends never talk to Frank about his writing. If only Connie could help him. She should remember what it was like. But she seems scared to talk to him any more, keeps coming up with excuses. The only thing she's done so far is give him those bloody diaries which he's been too afraid to admit possession of to Frank. That must have been what's scared her off – maybe she's only just realised her affair could be uncovered. Martin realises he's stalking around the room.

Fucking Frank. What else has he got hidden away? Sometimes he thinks the rival biographer in Hamilton has got the right idea, not even trying to talk to the bugger. Frank just confuses him more, refuses certain subjects, scoffs at what others say, all the time leading him on with promises of treasure, only to lock it away as soon as Martin gets a glimpse of a glitter.

Martin trips over one of the piles of books by his desk and they scatter and shoot across the floor. He swears. He can hear Alice upstairs, calling something. Just go away. He squats down and picks the books off the floor, stroking their covers gently, as if to soothe them. Henry James, James Joyce, Oscar Wilde, Virginia Woolf, Henry Miller, Ernest Hemingway, Evelyn Waugh, William

Faulkner, Edith Wharton, George Orwell. Such great writers.

Alice comes in to find Martin sitting on the floor, books all around him, head in his hands.

'What's wrong? Martin?'

He looks up at her, eyes blurred, such an ache in his chest.

'I don't know what I'm doing, Alice.'

She comes over and crouches down beside him, pushing books out of the way with her foot, raising a hand uncertainly to his cheek.

'Tell me. What's wrong?'

'It's that bloody Frank.'

Why should he feel this – this emptiness, this yearning?

'What about Frank?'

He tries to explain. He knows she won't understand.

'He's just not . . . not worth it. Do you know what I mean?' It hurts to raise his eyes to hers. 'The biography. He's not a worthy subject. He's just a rotten old prick.'

Alice clears away a few more books and sits down next to him, puts an arm around his shoulder. He wants to shake her off.

'Martin, do you remember when you first wanted to write a biography of Frank? You remember then I asked you why? Why Frank Finnigan?'

His shoulders stiffen. She always has to be fucking right.

'Yeah, I remember.'

'What did you say? You said you wanted to do something on Frank because no one else had done one, because he's a world-wide bestseller, he's one of the most significant writers this country has ever produced, but he's dismissed as a populist.'

Alice's arm slips off to rest on the floor. Martin exhales.

'If it's too hard, leave it. Why are you so wound up about him?'

'I. . . I don't know. That's the problem, I don't know bloody anything.'

Alice sighs. Her green eyes are dark like a sea at night.

'It's just a phase. That's what John says. You'll get over it.'

'Who the hell asked John?'

'I did. He *is* a psychologist.'

'It's none of his bloody business. Jesus, what have you been saying to him?'

The bastard, he's at the source of all this. He feels the anger surge into his blood, his quickening heart pump it around his body.

Alice draws her arms into herself.

'We talk mainly about me actually. At least he cares enough to ask about me, to check how my life is going. He's just being a good friend.'

'Is he your friend or your psychologist?' He's almost spitting. 'Because he can't be both.'

Alice stands up slowly.

'You better get to work. Lance and I will be over at my parents'.'

She sounds angry, but the door closes softly behind her.

Martin picks himself up off the floor. His limbs are aching with tension, his chest is tight. At least she's gone now. He stretches slowly, goes to sit at the desk. He must do this. Must. Forget why, just do it. Fuck John. He can have her. He reads over the last few pages, scribbles a few notes down the margin, writes a couple of paragraphs, and pauses. Some quote is needed now. He looks through his card catalogue and finds the reference he wants, turns to page 82.

'The ferment of genius is quickly imparted and when a man is great he makes others believe in greatness. By that token one's life is altered. One has climbed a hill, looked out and over and the valley of one's own condition will be forever greener.'

This is what he must aim for. He can no longer bear to remain in this dry and dusty valley yellowing before him.

Chapter 7

'Stories are less about facts and more about meanings.'

Martin is about to leave, is packing the tape recorder into his satchel, next to his notebook with the questions neatly printed out, all organised and absolutely ready for him this time, when Alice comes in holding the phone.

'It's his wife.'

She hands him the phone, stands there, watching him with an inscrutable expression. She's been making sure she gets to answer first since he hung up on John the other day.

'Connie?'

'Hello, Martin.' Her voice is thin and wavery, stretched out and flattened through the telephone wires. 'Frank asked me to ring.'

He can't hear her very well. She sounds like she's whispering. He turns his back on Alice.

'Yes?'

'You can't come today. He's not well.'

Martin feels his heart double-skip. He's been waiting for days for this appointment, the last one before the enforced break of Christmas. Alice has insisted they go to his parents again this year, although they went there last time. He doesn't even want to see his parents, he'd rather they saw hers – at least they'd still be in Wellington. She's just being unreasonable. Again. And now this. He can feel Alice still standing there behind him, listening.

'That's no good, Connie. What's wrong with him?'

'He's coming down with the 'flu. I'm afraid you'll have to put it off until after Christmas.'

It'll be two weeks before he gets back from Blenheim. He'll go mad. There's too much he needs to sort out before he can get on to the next chapter.

'How about if I just come round to talk to you? I've got a few questions I still need cleared up.'

'No, I don't think so.'

'We could talk about your own writing if you like. I've been reading your last book of poetry, it's very good.'

'No, Martin.'

'Well perhaps I'll ring tomorrow to check how he is, shall I?'

'No.' The thin voice tightens, taut as a piano string. 'I'll get him to ring you when he's better.'

'What about Ian? Can I speak to Ian?'

He's been looking forward to meeting the son, home for Christmas holidays.

'He's not here right now. I'll ring you later.'

And there's a click and a burr as the line cuts off. Martin looks up at Alice. She'll just love this.

'I can't go there today, Frank's not well.'

'Shame.' Her chin jutted hard, hand on hip in a sharp unforgiving angle, contradicts the sentiment of the word.

Martin sighs loudly. It's the worst December he can remember.

'I suppose you'll come out to the bay with me and Lance then,' Alice asks.

He flicks his eyes to the floor, hesitating, wondering how to phrase it. He should be going over the letters and journals again. He's wasted too much time already. His extended sabbatical only runs until the end of March.

Alice turns and leaves the room, and he imagines her growling under her breath. Done it again. But she's back, this time both hands propped on defiant hips.

'In that case, Lance and I may stay at Eastbourne for a few days.

Leave you alone with your precious book. There's plenty of food in the fridge.'

And she's gone again. Thank God. He'll be able to get on with it at last. Maybe he could even get out of Blenheim – but no, that would cause real fireworks.

Martin dumps the bag back by his desk and sits down, opens up the letters file, humming. He likes the letters most, actually. Frank shines through them clearly, much less opaque than in the fiction and even, Martin feels, more truthfully than in his own journals. Here is the real Frank, rude and cantankerous, thoughtful and pontificating, with a description so sharp, more poignant than in his writing, which is sometimes pompous, trying too hard for effect. The letters are written quickly, capturing passing moods. Martin can hear Frank's voice behind them as he reads.

Joseph,

Sorry for not replying to your letter earlier, but it's been so bloody hectic here what with the launch and all the associated bullshit. Sam Cash and Lovelock made the trip down and seemed to enjoy themselves, getting stuck into the old amber liquid. Shame you couldn't join us. You would have loved my speech, I really wowed them. Glad you liked the book though – it turned out quite different from how I described last spring, didn't it? But I think that's the way it should be. That's where novelists like Skidmore differ from me, they've got the thing all cut and dried before they even pick up a pen, and you can tell it. The words taste stale. In all the best books the writer is discovering the story as he goes along, just as the reader is. Not that the reviewers understand any of that. You'll have seen the great Kiwi clobbering machine is already well in action. Bloody idiots, one day I'll be recognised and they'll all have to eat their mealy-mouthed weasel words. As for your difficulty getting hold of a copy, I don't wonder. Alex tells me Whitcombe and Tombs refuse to display it, as it's their policy not to feature any book produced in NZ that's not printed by them. They do stock copies but, as you discovered, you only get them if you persist. Perhaps I should move out of this backwater country altogether.

In the meantime, if you're still planning on coming to stay, come soon. We're putting the house on the market at the end of the year. I'm determined to go through with the move to Nelson, although Connie's still not happy about it. She'll come right, once we're over there and settled, but in the meantime she's going crook, and spending a lot of time sulking over at her sister's or somewhere. Don't let this put you off coming, I could do with the company.

Had to pause there as the doorbell just went. The priest, would you believe, looking for Connie. I made the mistake of inviting him in, though Con's out at the moment, and we stood in the lounge for some time talking about the weather. He wouldn't sit down, silly bugger, just stood there, fidgeting and picking at his great hairy ears. He spotted my mug of beer sitting on the table next to this letter, and his eyes kept drifting over to it like he couldn't believe anyone could be drinking the dreaded alcohol at half past two in the afternoon. In the end I couldn't stand it anymore and lit up my pipe just to expel him from the house entirely. What the hell Connie wanted with such a ning-nong is beyond me.

Anyway Joe, write soon and let me know when you can come. We'll paint the town together. I'm working nights at the moment, and writing during the mornings, but I can arrange to swap shifts whenever necessary, so just let me know. Send our love to Susan et al.

Frank

August 1968. The tone changes after the move to Nelson in early '69. Frank's forty-two then, writing full-time for the first time, but he seems to have lost confidence. What's different?

Mack,

Thanks for your letter, it's good to hear the old hacks are still going strong. I miss the news business now and again and find plenty of excuses to go down to the *Evening Mail* to catch up on what's going on.

I knew you'd laugh at the idea of me writing leaders but the money, small as it is, is much needed. And I'm enjoying the challenge, although have to admit to being a little out of touch with the local issues here. And I do mean 'local' – this is a real small town!

The writing itself is not going so well. I scratch away every day and likely as not screw it up again the next. I face up in the morning to a blank sheet of paper and sweat it out, but find myself unable to work more than a few hours at a time with little to show for it. In Wellington I imagined writing full-time would be just that – eight-hour days with reams of manuscript churning out, like raw meat transformed into sausages. I'm gradually discovering some remedies for my lack of ability but never imagined it would be such hard yacker. I always believed I had more material than was ever possible to write, and this sudden paucity makes me wonder if I'll write anything worthwhile again. Maybe I've abandoned my career in journalism and the guaranteed income for an idiotic dream.

Those are the worst times but, as Connie keeps telling me, it's still early days. She has settled in much better than she expected – much better than I, in fact. She's made a number of good friends already – I think you know one of them, Jill Steele. They're often out and about together. The kids seem quite happy too. So there's no need to despair just yet. I'll keep plugging on and hope it comes to something. Otherwise you can expect us back in Wellington before too long!

Frank

Jill Steele: JS. That possibility hadn't occurred to him, but it does make sense. No wonder Frank sounds down. But he can't know about the affair yet. Martin goes through the rest of the letters – it's not until much later that Frank seems back to his old obnoxious self. The arrogance begins to appear again in 1970, once he starts working on *The Game of the Few*. Frank's tone is more easy again, more relaxed – the letters from Elena even remark on the fact. Here's one dated March 11, 1970.

It's good to hear you are feeling more content, my dear, more 'chipper' as you say. (I will never get used to these strange New Zealand expressions.) I had to ring you after receiving your letter on Wednesday, it was such a shock. But I believe it has released something in you and now you will be able to go on and write as you were meant to. I truly believe this is the way through this. Write, my darling. Write it out and ease your heart.

The date is soon after Frank's discovery of Connie's 'secret activities'; perhaps that's what she's referring to. He should ask Frank – but he can't now, damn it. Elena's 'darling' makes him wonder about their relationship, too – maybe Frank had an affair in retaliation. If only he could see the letters Frank wrote to Elena. But there's no way the Queen of France will hand them over. If she still has them. He asked once, and she said they were burned. Still, he didn't believe her. It might be worth another go. If he can't go see Frank, he might as well try cracking the Ice Queen again. He reaches for his jacket.

She comes to the door and peers at him through the bevelled glass. Martin can see her outline, a thin woman edged in purple, a mound of grey hair piled on top of her head.
'Who is it?'
'It's Martin Wrightson.'
'Who?'
Elena opens the door and the blank face sharpens to a pointed little nose, still shapely cheekbones dusted with powder, and piercing blue eyes blinking rapidly at him. A tendril of her long hair loosens and falls down across her neck, exposed. For a second, Martin feels like putting an arm around her, gathering her up in a bundle, but the fierce eyes prevent any tenderness. He remembers what she said last time and straightens up.

'You might remember I came to see you a few months ago. I'm Martin, I'm doing the biography of Frank Finnigan.'

'Yes, yes. I remember you.'

And she turns, swoops back into the depths of the house, leaving him peering into the dark, empty corridor. Presumably he's meant to follow. He creeps uncertainly along the hallway, a small insect enticed into a predator's lair. She's in the kitchen, making tea.

'Asseyez-vous. Sit down, sit down.'

Martin pulls a wooden chair out from the farmhouse kitchen table and perches uncertainly. The afternoon sun is playing along the old dishes propped on the hutch dresser, licking at the colours. Elena sets the teapot down heavily, a splash of liquid spilling in a little pool between them. Martin watches her select two cups from the dresser and place them on the table, lift the hefty pot once more.

'I'll do it.'

The glare forces him to his seat again, and he holds his breath as he watches the wavery line of tea sway and bend in a drunken path to his cup. He waits until she sits and pours her own.

'Frank's not well,' he says.

The purple eyes widen, and her hand, bruised with age, shakes against the saucer.

'What's wrong with him? Has he, is he . . . what is wrong? Tell me quickly.'

Shit.

'No, no. He's fine really. Just a bit of 'flu, that's all.'

'You scare me, you silly boy. What have you come here for?'

'I can't talk to him, and I need to talk to you.'

Her hand waves in a gesture of dismissal, rubs angrily at the side of a crinkled eye.

This has been a mistake.

'I told you last time. People always come bothering, asking silly questions about dear Frank. I'm not telling you, I said before. I won't tell you.'

'Who's been coming here?'

He thinks of his Hamilton rival.

'I won't tell anyone. Nobody keeps secrets these days. Well, Elena Lerner, she knows when to keep her mouth shut. What did Frank tell you? Did he tell you to come see me?'

'No . . .'

'There you are, then. You are just another busy-body.'

For a minute the accent obscures the word and he wonders if she's swearing at him in French. He drinks his tea, crosses his legs, taps the edge of the yellow checked tablecloth. He's sick of these games.

'I don't know how I'm meant to write anything about the bloody man if nobody will tell me anything. All I know is what Frank tells me, and we all know how expert he is at fiction.'

He feels like a petulant child, kicking his heels under his grandmother's kitchen table. Elena is lifting her head and laughing, her face falling into a much younger light. She is beautiful. Martin drains his cup. Fuck it.

'So tell me about your affair.'

The laughing stops and she lowers her head, levels her gaze at him, blinking the sparkles away, darkening her irises like a dangerous sea on the turn. She must be seventy, but she is formidable. A very French formidable.

'You remind me of Frank, Mar-teen.'

He likes the way she says his name, the vowels rounded, exotic, flavoured with Europe.

'You think you know things about people, don't you? You think you have other people all worked out, you know the way the world works. What you say things are, they are. Well, darlink, you know nothing.'

She fumbles in her cardigan pocket and brings out a slim packet of cigarettes, deftly draws one out and lights it.

'I can tell you about our affair, oui, c'est vrai. I loved Frank, still love him. He is one of my darlinks. A foolish man, but my darlink. I'm sure he would tell you about our affair too, if you asked him. You haven't, have you?'

Martin keeps his eyes on the tablecloth.

'You see, it is not important. Our friendship is important, oui, our love. But the physical, that is just passion. It comes, it goes. Constance knows about us, you need not worry.'

Connie knows?

'They have a very interesting relationship, don't you think? I admire her greatly, the way she has handled it all. You see, she knows Frank, she really knows his mind. I know his heart. But she, she knows all those things that go on inside his head. That doesn't interest me so, you know. What interests you, Monsieur Wrightson? What is it you are looking for?'

'If I knew that, I don't think I would be here.'

She laughs again, that beautiful young girl's laugh, Paris in the spring time.

'I think you may be closer than you know.'

She stubs the cigarette out in a porcelain ashtray, gets up and leaves the room. Martin stays motionless, bent forward in the wooden chair, eyes full of yellow checks, heavy with the sun colour, so heavy. He wishes he could drop his head down on the cloth, but he cannot move.

Martin picks his head up from the desk and goes through the letters in the shoe box once more. He's sure some are missing. One at least. The dates don't match up. There are pieces in this puzzle that look too new, fit too perfectly. And some of these gaps he despairs of ever being able to fill. Wednesday March 7, 1970. He knows Frank wrote to Elena on that date, but it's certainly not among the letters she's given him, passing them to him in a quick, underhand gesture at the front door as he was leaving. He checks through the dates again. There is love here, illicit, a minor scandal, but not what he's been looking for. There's something else.

He ties the soft purple ribbon around the letters and places them back in the box. He wishes he'd never seen them. It's too confusing. He's sick of trying to piece together this picture. He leaves the shoebox in the middle of the desk and goes to bed, half hoping it may disappear overnight.

It begins to spit just before Martin reaches the Hataitai tunnel. He clicks the windscreen wipers on as the car is gathered into the grey clouds waiting for him on the other side, and turns towards the airport and Seatoun. The wipers whine back and forth, a metronome. He shouldn't have left the house like that, but he needed to get out. He just wishes Alice would stop trying to organise him – that's what makes him angry. There's no fucking way he's going to see John, and he can't believe she asked him to. That guy's really got her brainwashed. Why the hell did she decide on counselling in the first place? It seemed to start as simply something for her to do. Well, he wasn't being dragged into the mumbo-jumbo.

Martin parks the car outside Frank's house and gets out, stands a moment in the soft drizzle. There's a light on in the kitchen. Maybe he shouldn't have come. He wonders again what to say to Connie, what excuse to use. She won't like it. Too bloody bad. He takes the steps two at a time. Connie answers the door and Martin abandons all excuses.

'Hello, Connie. I've come to see Frank.'

She's flustered, stands there looking at him, her mouth slightly open, waiting for the words to fill it. She twists a damp tea towel nervously in her hands. Martin's surprised: he had expected anger, not this. He presses himself through the doorway.

'How's he feeling today? Still in bed?'

'No, no.' The tea towel twitches. 'I couldn't keep him there. He insists on getting up and writing. I think he's in his study now. You stay here and I'll go and see if he's available.'

She pushes him into the lounge. *Available.* Martin paces in front of the windows. The sea is a long grey whale gliding past.

'Hello there, old chap. So you could come after all. Excellent. I've been missing you. Sit down and Connie will make us some tea.'

Connie is nowhere in sight.

'You seem very well. How's your health?'

'Fit as a buck-rat.'

Martin frowns. 'Connie told me you were sick yesterday.'

'Did she? Oh, well, yes. Yesterday I wasn't feeling quite myself.'

Martin doesn't believe him.

'Sit down, anyway, boy. Tell me what you've been up to. You've missed Ian, I'm afraid. He's out somewhere or other – hate to think where. How's chapter seven?'

'Slow.'

'Ah, well. That's the way it goes sometimes. Anything I can help you with?'

'You haven't found any more of the letters from when you lived in Nelson, have you?'

'No, no, can't say I have. You're lucky to have as many as I gave you. We threw out a lot of stuff in the move.'

'Any other letters from Elena Lerner?'

'Elena. No. Why?'

'I'm sure there are some missing. The dates don't match up entirely.'

'You'll just have to do without them.'

'Yes.'

The rain taps on the glass, a persistent visitor demanding entry.

'I went to see Elena yesterday.'

'Yes, she told me.'

Martin feels deflated. He should have guessed she would tell him; but now his advantage is gone, Frank is ahead of him yet again. He's silent.

'So I suppose you want to hear all about the affair? You needn't sulk because I didn't tell you. It's a private thing, between me and her. I didn't want it splashed in front of the world, cheapened. But now you know, ask me what you like. I'll answer.'

Martin can't think of what to ask.

'You remind me of my son, you know. Sullen son of a prick.'

Martin glares at him. 'You being the prick.'

'Have you got eye trouble?'

His glare narrows further. He's in no mood for it today.

Frank sighs, gets up and goes out of the room, and comes back with a couple of beers.

'Connie's disappeared and I can't be bothered making tea.'

Martin shifts and takes the beer, grunting in gratitude, feeling slightly foolish.

'All right, here it is. Elena and I had been friends a long time. I worked with her husband Michael at PA, but he died in '68. When we moved back to Wellington we saw a lot of each other. She's a great reader, you know. She'd read my manuscripts and tell me what she thought. And she was usually right on the button too, Elena.'

He sits down again, leans his head back and tilts the can up. A golden rivulet zigzags down his chin, is caught with a stubby finger.

'She was beautiful. Still is, don't you think? So elegant, sensual. The sex was . . . natural. It was just . . . right. We fitted together, soul mates if you like. No, that's balls, taking it too far.'

He slams the can on the table, slaps his thigh in disgust. 'You see why I didn't want to talk to you about it? It changes everything. When I talk to you, the person becomes smaller, less alive. She becomes a painted picture, a character in one of my books, not the woman I loved – I love. I can't do it, Martin. Don't make me do it.'

He covers his face with his hand.

'Does Connie know?'

'Yes, yes.' The hand sweeps over his hair and the old man glares at Martin, insulted. 'You don't get it at all, do you?'

'Elena told me I was like you.'

'Did she?'

And he's just an old man again, sitting awkwardly, his expression caught between pleasure and choler.

'I'm not sure it was a compliment.'

For a moment Martin wonders if Frank might slap him, but Frank's face muscles slacken, and he starts to chuckle, hack hacking into a rasping cough. Worried, Martin hands him the beer can, and stands over him as he pours it down, his heaving subsiding.

'I've got something for you,' he finally coughs out. 'Not letters. But I did find something the other day which you'll like.'

Frank goes out of the room, and Martin hears him thumping heavily down the stairs. His chest is hollow. He feels afraid.

Frank reappears, waving two books triumphantly at him.

'The missing diaries!'

'What? But I have all your diaries.'

'No, remember I couldn't find these ones: 1970, 1971. Here you go, boy. The missing links. That will cheer you up.'

1970, 1971. The ones that Connie had given him secretly. So what on earth are these?

Martin's standing out on the balcony, his fists clenched around the railing, just like when he was a kid. It's ridiculous, but he feels like a smoke. He's never smoked in his life. Fucking Christmas. She hadn't even let him bring any work over.

He hears the squeak of the screen door behind him and his

hold tightens. He looks out at the dark sky, the stars.

'I can't do this any more, Martin,' Alice says.

He's not going to turn around for her. It's all just clichés, psychobabble.

'If you really don't want to be here, let's go back to Wellington.'

He turns. 'You mean it?'

'I can't stand watching you treat your parents like this.'

'They're my parents. I'll treat them how I want to treat them. You don't know how they've treated me.' He stalks down the end of the balcony, crashes his shoulder against the post.

'Well I don't want Lance to see it. John says it's not good for him.'

'John?' He stalks back to stand in front of her. 'What the hell does John know about Lance?'

Her eyes flash green. He can just hear the words under her breath.

'More than you do.'

He knew it. He knew she wouldn't be able to resist bringing up that incident again.

'Listen, I told you what happened wasn't my fault.'

'Yes, you told me.' Alice is getting angry. 'Apparently it's the fault of an eight-year-old boy if his father forgets to pick him up from the swimming baths.'

'I told you . . .'

'Two hours, Martin. He waited there for two hours before catching that bus.'

'Well he's old enough to be able to catch a bus, isn't he?'

'It went to Karori! I had to go and pick him up at the bus terminal!'

'Well he shouldn't have told me he was going over to his friend's place after swimming, should he? I didn't think he needed to be picked up.'

His left eyelid is pulsing with the words. It's a lie. They both know it.

'This is not about you and me, Martin. This is about Lance. You betrayed your son.'

It's all so over the top. He knows who that is. He pushes his face angrily against hers.

'I suppose that's what John says, isn't it? And I suppose John thinks it's better for you to leave me. Maybe he thinks you both should go live with him now, is that it?'

'No.'

Alice moves backwards, her hands pushing out to keep him back. She looks frightened. It feels good.

'Maybe it would be better if we moved out for a while, gave you some space.'

'Oh it's all so predictable.'

He shoves his hands in his pockets. He's not going to hit her, it's not worth it. Martin feels a coldness settling within him. It makes him shiver and his eyes blink.

'When we get back to Wellington, Lance and I will go stay at Eastbourne.'

Her skirt flares and the screen door slams behind her.

Martin opens the two 1970 diaries and lays them flat on his desk, next to each other, like twins in a crib. They're fraternal. While there are many differences in appearance – one has dark hair, the other blond; one blue eyes, his brother brown; one smiles, the other does not – it is the subtle differences in personality that interest Martin. And of course, the two periods of time when their histories diverge so markedly. Interesting that he chose to keep the discovery of Connie's affair, although it's not clear it was another woman. And yet some of the paragraphs omitted seem completely innocuous. Martin runs his finger down the spine of each book. Here at last is his secret. He reads a section of the new journal that Frank's given him.

The anger's gone now, only a thin residue remains. I've been such a damned blind fool. But I've been working too hard, and it's only natural Connie gets lonely. I forgive her and we've agreed not to speak of it again. We are both very loving again. I couldn't do it without her.

Meanwhile, I started work on the book today. It's very exciting and I am determined to work hard and fulfil its potential. The story has so many layers, it is so complex. The characters too I imagine very fully. I like the main character Rex, flawed as he ultimately is. But aren't we all? And isn't that what makes a reader respond, recognising one's own frailties? The workings of his inner life – this is just as important as the plot movement, the discoveries of deception and counter-deception. Here is the <u>meaning</u>. Stories are less about facts and more about meanings. The story should expose his world as illusion, while lyrically celebrating its power.

I feel different. After all those days fretting, sitting in front of a blank sheet of paper, wasting time. Now I'm ready to work.

I think it was the illness that snapped me out of it. The other week I spent four days in bed, running a high fever. I'm grateful for it now, of course, because it was during those wild nights of tossing and turning, forehead burning up, that I first got the idea for this new book. I envisioned Rex Widdens as a child first, hating his family in the way only a child can, watching his brother's face as the car slowly toppled and fell. The next morning, with a temperature of 103, I saw a man who was a spy, fleeing from a Russian mansion, secrets tucked into his breast pocket. Later I recognised him as the child I had seen earlier, grown up. By then the complicated plot movements were beginning to wind themselves around my head. When I awoke the following day, I realised the man was a double agent and suddenly it all made sense. However, the allegory only became plain once I was fully recovered and reviewing the notes I had made of my dreams. The 'uncovering' of this story has been amazing to me. It has come so complete and wholly visioned, quite unlike any of my previous books. I believe it will be great and my first real success.

Contrast the journal which Connie gave him.

The anger's mainly gone now, only a thin residue remains, will always remain. But that wasn't the only gift. The other I would never have expected either. Such a fool, a damned blind fool. I'm going to take it. I surely deserve something from her. I've decided that's my due. We've agreed not to speak of it again.

Connie has been very loving today. She knows full well the second discovery of her secret activities has had as much impact as the first. I keep wanting to ask her about it, how she planned it all, went about it, whether she went through similar agonies to mine. If she did, it doesn't show. I'm full of admiration for her, but have to admit to strokes of jealousy. I look at her in a new light now. Sometimes I catch myself looking at her, wondering how it could be I could know so little about the woman I loved, the woman I married, the wife who has borne my children. It excites me, yet also fills me with fear. If I don't know her, how can I know anybody? Do I know myself?

I started work on the book today. This also provokes excitement and fear. It's so unlike any of my published fiction, I'll have to work hard on it. I'm determined to fulfil its potential. The story has so many layers, it's quite exquisitely complex. The characters too are very full, although they could do with some sharpening and I think Rex Widdens is sometimes a little clichéd. I like him, though, flawed as he ultimately is. But aren't we all? And isn't that what makes a reader respond, recognising one's own frailties? The workings of his inner life – this is just as important as the plot movement, the discoveries of deception and counter-deception. Here is the <u>meaning</u>. I grasp that better, I believe. Stories are less about facts and more about meanings. The story exposes his world as illusion, while lyrically celebrating its power.

I feel different. All those days fretting, sitting in front of a blank sheet of paper. A real no-hoper, just wasting time. But now I have this to work on, to use as a base, I can see this will be my salvation. Connie can see it too. Nowadays she doesn't go anywhere, just keeps around the house, does the garden, cooks the meals, looks after the children. Atonement. We'll see about that.

I keep to my study, working. The children don't interest me at the moment. They're always wanting something, always interrupting. She can have them – she was the one who wanted them after all. I'd like to go away for a while, just take the book to work on, some little hidey-hole in the Marlborough Sounds perhaps. But there's no money, no hidey-hole to escape to. Here she has to watch me work. I hope it hurts.

She says she loves me still. I don't know if I love her. I don't feel very loving and I don't feel very loveable.

Funny, it reminds me of my own parents. When did they first move into separate rooms? I remember catching Dad with Molly once when I was very young. They didn't know I was there. I'd run home from school early and didn't think anyone would be home. When I heard noises coming from the bedroom I crept to the door. My father was naked, pumping away at her pushed-up skirts as Molly lay on the bed, her face turned away from the door. I mentioned it to my father the next day, simply as a matter of interest, although I must have known enough not to mention it to mother. He told me fiercely that I must have been dreaming. This left me confused and I tried to explain further, but he cut me off with a terrible slap. I didn't dare risk telling anyone else what I'd seen, for fear something more awful would happen. I think I have felt guilty about sex ever since. Well, there's been nothing to feel guilty about for a while. She can take the blame for that.

There's a section here that's been crossed out. Martin struggles to read it but can make out only a phrase or two. He sighs and gives up. Cunning old bastard. How much else has been fake? The letters? The anecdotes? A complete fucking lie. Frank hadn't reckoned on Martin, though. He will find the truth and expose it to the world, and Frank will realise he has seriously underestimated him. There's something big going on here, for Frank to go to so much effort to cover it up. He suspects . . . but, no. No, he shouldn't be hasty, no jumping to conclusions. He will go through it all, gather as much evidence as he can, and then confront the nasty old prick. He imagines the moment: Frank with tears in his eyes, nodding in contrition. More likely he'll have a good laugh, one of those long, hacking convulsions, and then pretend it's been some kind of test.

Martin rises from his seat in anger and goes to the door, then turns and hurries back to the desk, grabs one of the journals and marches out to the phone in the corridor.

'I want to talk to him.'

'He's not very well today, Martin.'

'Connie, for Christ's sake, you know I don't believe you any more. Just get the bastard on the phone.'

'But, really, I mean it. He isn't well.'

'I don't care.'

There's a long silence, then a clatter as if someone is picking up the handpiece.

'Martin?'

'Frank. I've been reading the diary you gave me.'

'Oh, yes. Look, Martin, can this wait? I'm not feeling too good.'

'I just wanted to thank you for giving it to me. A lot of people wouldn't have, you know. They would've pretended they'd lost it or something. There's lots of great stuff in it that I'll be able to use. Real revelations.'

Grunt.

'I especially liked the bit about your father.'

'My Dad?'

'Yes, you know, the bit where you describe seeing him having sex with the home help when you were a child.'

Pause.

'I don't remember.'

'You know. Here, I'll read it: "When I heard noises coming from the bedroom I crept to the door. My father was naked, pumping away at her pushed-up skirts as Molly lay on the bed, her face turned away from the door. I mentioned it to my father the next day, simply as a matter of interest, although I must have known enough not to mention it to mother. He told me fiercely that I must have been dreaming. This left me confused and I tried to explain further, but he cut me off with a terrible slap. I didn't dare risk telling anyone else what I'd seen, for fear something more awful would happen. I think I have felt guilty about sex ever since."'

He can hear Frank breathing on the other end.

'So thank you again. Thank you very much.'

The breathing is laboured, rasping.

'Frank? Are you all right?'

There's no reply, just that ghastly wheezing.

'I've got a few questions to ask you about some of it, though. How about we arrange a time to meet?'

The phone clicks off and a shrill tone buzzes in his ear. Martin replaces the receiver and smiles.

That's got the bugger worried.

Chapter 8

'Believe it or not, Martin, you're not family.'

Martin hears the phone ringing inside as he struggles to find the front door key, his arms full of groceries. He puts in the wrong key, swears and drops a bag of fruit and vegetables. He hears the answerphone pick up. Bloody shopping. He wishes Alice would come back. He finds the right key at last and stumbles into the hallway, skidding on the rug. He hears Connie's voice in the distance, eerily echoing down the hall.

'I wish I knew what the hell you said to him.'

The answerphone clicks off. Martin feels his Adam's apple bob tightly up and down his throat. Connie never swears. He slows down and brings all the shopping bags in before going to the phone. The little red light is blinking insistently. He presses play.

'Martin, it's Connie. I'm ringing to say Frank's in hospital. He's had a stroke.' The voice trembles very slightly, pauses. 'The doctors say it's a minor stroke. It was on Sunday, just after you were talking to him on the phone. I came out of the kitchen to find him sitting in the corridor clutching his head, then he fell over unconscious. By the time an ambulance arrived he'd come round again, but he's partially paralysed. He's in Wakefield Hospital, Ward 5. He can talk; he's sitting up, asking for people to come and visit. He asked for you. That's why I'm calling.'

The unspoken words ring clearly in the silence.

'Anyway, he wants you to come. I wish I knew what the hell you said to him.'

Martin sits down on the chair next to the phone table. His finger wavers over the play button but he thinks better of it. He doesn't want to hear that accusatory tone again. A stroke. Jesus. That was three days ago. Could it have been something to do with what he said? Pretending Frank had given him the real diary? But Frank had said he was ill before that. It was just a coincidence.

Martin slumps forward, his head in his hands. He imagines Frank sitting like that.

Martin waits at the reception desk where a young nurse is on the phone. There is a faint smell of lavender. You'd hardly know it was a hospital, it's so quiet and pleasant. Not like the place where Alice works, with the noise, the peeling paint, the stench of antiseptic overlying a deeper, more pervading smell of sickness. He fidgets a little. At least he needn't worry about running into Alice. But he's always been afraid of hospitals. He remembers being brought to visit his uncle in hospital when he was very young and getting lost on the way back from the toilet. The long snifter-green corridors, the stainless-steel trolleys piled high with starched linen, that smell of sickness, the rising panic.

The nurse gets off the phone and looks up at him, smiling. She has nice green eyes.

'Mr Finnigan? He's in room 13, just down the hall and to your left.'

Martin walks in the direction she indicates, and checks the numbers on the doors, glimpsing patients in a few of the rooms beyond. An old woman glares at him, her pink nightie gaping open to reveal a withered blue breast. He hurries on.

Thirteen.

Frank lies on the high hospital bed, asleep, the corner of his mouth sagging. He doesn't look much different; older somehow. His long arms resting on the tight white sheets are like an old man's, pale and blotchy. He is an old man, Martin thinks. He notices Connie as she stirs in a seat on the far side of the room, and turns to her. They look at each other, the silent form of Frank lying between them. He goes over to her, a fresh anger building.

'Why didn't you tell me sooner?'

She stands up, flushed.

'Believe it or not, Martin, you're not family.'

And she leaves the room.

The focus for his emotion lost, Martin turns uncertainly to the sleeping man. He brings a chair up to the bed and sits beside him, wonders if he should touch Frank, hold his hand. But can't bring himself to. He sits there, hunched, miserable, and tries not to cry. A trickle of saliva dribbles from the sagging corner of Frank's mouth and he smacks his lips together, one eye opening. Martin nearly stands up in alarm.

'Who's there?' Frank's looking towards the door. 'Who's there?'

Martin feels a fear himself at Frank's note of fright, and leans forward over him, hands on his.

'It's Martin. It's okay, Frank. It's Martin.'

'Martin.'

Frank turns his head towards him and Martin sees there's something wrong with his eyes. One of the eyelids is not fully open, the other looks at him glassily.

'Can you see me?'

'No. Not really. I know your voice though, Martin, I'd know your voice anywhere. The doctors say the sight might come back. They think some of the symptoms may be temporary. I'll come right, don't you worry.'

Martin feels a sinking inside.

'What are the other effects?'

'Can't move my arm or leg much, that's all really. It's the left side, luckily. Didn't get my writing arm. And I haven't gone cuckoo yet, so that's something. Getting sick of this place though, everyone fussing round.'

Sounds like Frank. Martin wonders if he should apologise for upsetting him on the phone, edges around it.

'When did it happen?'

'Sunday, they tell me. But I must admit I can't remember the weekend at all. Last thing I remember was watching tele Friday night. It happened sudden as anything – well, they do apparently, these things. But the docs say they're not always as bad as they first appear, and I've got a good chance at complete recovery.'

The false optimism is obvious, and Frank stumbles over it.

'Walt Whitman had a stroke, you know, ten years before *Leaves of Grass*. Tell me what you've been doing anyway. How's the book?'

'Oh, you know. Slowly but surely.'

'That reminds me, I found another box of stuff for you, something you've been looking for. You must ask Connie for it.'

He's grinning lopsidedly. Martin, embarrassed, can think of nothing to say.

'And how's the family? That wife of yours?'

Even more at a loss, Martin mumbles something blandly positive. He can't remember Frank having asked after his family before.

'Did you see Connie? Is Connie still here?'

Again, that potential panic underlying the words, threatening to break through and escape into the room.

'Yes, Connie's here. She's just gone to have a break.'

'Right. She's got the kids coming over, you know. I said not to worry them but she insisted. Ian's arriving tomorrow, I think. You haven't met Ian, have you?

'No.'

'You'll like him. No need for him to come, of course, the doctors say I'll be sky blue soon.'

'Sky blue?'

'What?'

'You said the doctors said you'd be sky blue.'

They're silent for a moment. Martin notices Frank's right hand shaking a little.

'Can I get you anything? Would you like a drink?'

The ghostly eye searches around his head.

'No, no thanks, Martin. I'm right.'

A nurse comes in and nods at Martin, talks over loudly to Frank.

'I've just come to take your blood pressure, Mr Finnigan.'

She lifts his right arm and rolls up the flimsy hospital gown to reveal a freckled white shoulder, a puff of grey hair peeking from the armpit. Frank's eyebrows lower to a familiar frown, making Martin smile.

'They're always doing this, it's a bloody nuisance.'

'Come on, you old grump. Won't take a minute.'

'You needn't treat me like a child.'

'You needn't act like one.'

Martin is shocked by the slap, but the nurse is unperturbed.

'Right, if you're going to play up, I'll come back later.' She passes Connie in the doorway. 'Up to his games again, your husband. I'll be back in ten.'

Connie looks at Martin balefully.

'Perhaps you should go.'

'No, no, it was just that old bitch squeezing me too hard again. Stay, Martin, I promise I won't hit you.'

And there's the familiar laugh, wheezing rapidly this time into a cough. Frank leans back against the pillow and splutters, panting, his crooked mouth part open.

'I should go anyway.' Martin rises to his feet. 'Work to do, you know.' He pats Frank's hand again. It's cold.

'I'll get Connie to send you that box.'

'Thanks. I'll come back and see you later in the week. Maybe I'll bring some of the manuscript in to read to you.'

'Great. That'd be great.'

The words are thin and crumbling. Martin feels his eyes prick, and turns away, avoids Connie's gaze, murmurs a farewell. He goes back out to the reception and stands uncertainly a moment. The young green-eyed nurse sees him there.

'Found him all right, did you?'

'Yes, yes, thank you.'

'He's a bit of a character, our Mr Finnigan.'

He's not 'your' Mr Finnigan. He's Frank.

'Always a bit of a shock seeing them like that. Can I get you anything?'

Martin revives at her smile.

'Can you tell me a bit more about . . . what he's got.'

She leans her arms up on the counter, and the badge on her left breast burrows into her cardigan. He can see only the first three letters of her name. J U L. Julia?

'Sure. They told you it was a stroke, did they? The official name is ischemic cerebral infarction. It's basically caused by a sudden loss of blood supply to the brain. It can have very different symptoms, depending on the part of the brain affected. You'll have seen Mr Finnigan has muscular weakness on his left leg, arm and face, with some loss of vision. But the doctors are quite optimistic, they seem to think it was a minor blockage. It affected the thalamus, though.'

'The what?'

'The thalamus. It's at the base of the forebrain. It's an integrating centre – sort of a telephone switchboard, if you like. It processes all the incoming information, and the effects of a stroke there are quite unpredictable.'

She pauses. Martin decides he likes her; her straightforward manner comforts him. He wonders if Alice is like this at work.

'It can produce some bizarre symptoms, so we're keeping a close eye on him.'

Martin thinks on the conversation he had with Frank.

'I thought he seemed pretty normal, considering. He did mix up a word or two.'

'Sometimes communication is affected. We haven't noticed much of that with him yet. His wife was quite concerned about that possibility. She said he's a writer or something?'

'Yes. Have you not heard of him?'

'I don't read much. More of a movie fan, myself. Are you one of the family?'

'No, just a friend.'

There's a beeping noise behind the desk.

'Juliet, can you get that?'

'Excuse me.'

She bustles off down the hall. Juliet, then. Martin finds he's forgotten the way out. He asks a passing orderly who points back down to the right.

'Unless you're in the carpark? It's quicker to get to the carpark this way. Here, follow me.'

He takes Martin down the hallway towards Frank's room. As they pass 13, Martin looks in. Connie is leant over the bed, facing away, embracing Frank, who looks up towards Martin, unseeing, his right arm flung around her neck awkwardly, his face screwed up in a grimace of pain, tears running down his cheeks. Martin quickly looks away and follows behind the orderly, ashamed, as much as if he had burst in on his parents kissing. He shouldn't have come. He shouldn't see Frank like this. He walks slowly through the antiseptic corridors and outside to rows of cars glinting in the sunshine, trying to get the image of Frank's face out of his mind.

Martin takes a long time to answer the phone. It's a great effort simply to get up from his chair.

'It's Alice.'

'Hi.'

'Just thought I'd let you know I'll drop by today to pick up the rest of Lance's stuff as we discussed.'

'You don't have to ask permission.'

'I know. I'm just letting you know. Would you like me to bring Lance too?'

'Jesus, do I have book in time now to see him? Is that how it is?'

'Martin, you know very well how it is. Do you want me to bring him or not?'

It seems like an age since he's talked to her, yet it was only the other day. He'd like to see Lance. He misses him, misses them both. He mustn't yell at her.

'Yes, bring him. If he wants to come.'

'You're sounding very sorry for yourself today.'

'Frank's had a stroke.'

'What?'

'Frank's had a . . .'

'Oh, Martin. I'm so sorry.'

There's a long pause. Martin can't speak.

'Is it bad?'

'I'm not sure.'

Another pause.

'I almost feel like offering to come back.'

'But you don't.'

'Well. . .'

'Well why the hell would you?'

He replaces the receiver gently, with a quiet click, just as the doorbell goes. A man with a courier package stands on the front step. It's the box of material Frank had promised to send. Martin signs for it and takes it into his study; carefully splits the masking tape with a scalpel. There are some letters inside, originals, most of which he recognises as already having copies. A couple of short story drafts. At the bottom is a thick lump of messy paper that he pulls out with difficulty. The manuscript of *The Game of the Few*.

It's ten minutes before Martin realises he's crying.

❖ ❖ ❖

Martin stands at the door to room 13, confused. The bed's empty. Frank couldn't have been discharged: Connie asked him to come this morning while she goes to pick up Ian from the airport. The irises he's brought, the flowers tiny shrivelled purple hands, dangle limply in his arms. Then a man wearing a gaping hospital gown pushes past him and gets into Frank's bed.

'Excuse me, do you know where Frank Finnigan is?'

'Who?'

The young nurse he met last time, Juliet, comes up.

'Hello there. You looking for Mr Finnigan? He's been moved to room 17. Here, I'll show you.'

She takes Martin's elbow and turns him in the right direction, shepherding him like a patient.

'You'll find he's a bit worse today, I'm afraid.'

'Worse?'

'His memory's coming and going. You get that sometimes, when the thalamus is affected. You'll have to be patient with him. I'm just warning you. He may not know who you are.'

They reach room 17. The door is closed.

'Right, I'll leave you to it. Just go on in.'

Martin nods but waits until she leaves. He looks at the door. At its side, along the wall, are some pictures drawn by children. A happy golden sun beams down on some flowers, their bold petals stark and straight. Martin looks down at the irises in his hand and places them on a nearby chair. He takes a breath and opens the door.

Frank is propped up in the bed, in pyjamas this time. He turns towards the door, squinting.

'Is that you, Ian?'

Martin comes into the room and closes the door behind him.

'No, it's me. Martin.'

He goes up to the bed and stands before Frank. He smells like an old man. Martin remembers how he used to smell; he hadn't consciously registered it before: tobacco, of course. His hands and clothes smelt of tobacco, and there was something else, too, perhaps some sort of aftershave.

'Sit down, Ian.'

Martin doesn't bother correcting him. He sits down.

'I'm going to get straight to the point. Your mother tells me you're upset and you're thinking of leaving home, is that right?'

Frank's eyes are glassy, flickering around the shape of Martin's head. The left side of his mouth droops and his left arm lies still.

'It's not Ian, Frank. It's Martin.'

He reaches out to touch Frank's right hand, pats it reassuringly. Frank doesn't acknowledge the touch, or the words.

'I know your mother doesn't know what you're upset about, but I do. It's Elena, isn't it? I didn't think I'd have to spell it out to you like this. I thought you were old enough to understand, now you're sixteen.'

Martin's thrown by the way he addresses him. He feels uncomfortable, as if he's listening in on someone else's conversation. He mustn't trick Frank into revelations like this. He interrupts him.

'How are you feeling today, Frank? The doctors say you're getting better.'

'Doctors? What doctors? Who's that?'

'It's Martin, Frank. Martin Wrightson.' He almost adds 'your biographer', but feels presumptuous, as if this earlier Frank won't accept him.

'Martin, Martin.' He's mumbling now. 'I need a glass of water.'

Martin pours a glass from the jug on the bedside table and hands it to Frank, helping him grip it in his good hand.

'Someone's brought you flowers, I see.'

Dried flowers. Long stems with small hard yellow balls skewered at the end, brushed with bright yellow pollen. They look like yellow aniseed balls, or some other kind of sweet to be rolled around the mouths of children. Mixed in are stems from the honesty plant, delicate rice-paper pods, like soft veined skin.

Martin touches one between his fingers. He can hardly feel it at all. He rubs at it gently and the skin tears. Frank is holding the glass out to him. He takes it and sets it on the table, sits down beside him again.

'The book's coming along well. It's nearly finished. I'll bring some in and read it to you next time.'

He's lying. He hasn't done any work on the book for a week.

'Tomorrow blips the day whomever.'

'What?'

Frank doesn't repeat it. Martin shifts in his seat, tries to think of something to say. He's saved by Juliet.

'Hello, Mr Finnigan. Just come to check up on you again.'

She smiles at Martin encouragingly as she wraps a pad around Frank's upper arm. Martin clears his throat.

'He's looking better today, isn't he?'

She looks at him briefly, then back to the pump.

'Yes, we're doing just fine.'

Frank is lying back on the pillows with his eyes closed.

'Right, there we go. I'll come back and see you later on.'

Martin stands as she goes, and follows her to the door.

'Can I talk to you a moment?' he whispers.

'Sure.'

She motions him into the corridor and closes the door behind them.

'He thinks I'm his son, and it's twenty years ago.'

Her eyes are clear and green, with tiny yellow rings around the pupils.

'Yes, he's been getting mixed up with his timing. It might be best to go along with it, you know. Just humour him and he'll eventually come right on his own.'

'But . . . it feels wrong. It feels like I'm deceiving him.'

She pats his hand in a comforting gesture that Martin recognises he's used with Frank.

'It doesn't make much difference what we do, you know.'

She shrugs her small shoulders.

Martin notices tiny diamond studs glinting in her ears. He feels a childish impulse to touch them.

'Just do what you can, Mr . . .'

'Wrightson. Martin Wrightson.'

'Where's his wife today?'

'She's gone to the airport to pick up their son. He's coming over from Australia.'

'That's good. Familiar faces sometimes help jolt them out of it a bit. Why don't you just sit with him until they come, eh?'

He nods gloomily and goes back into the room. Frank's eyes are open again, his head turned towards the window.

'Beautiful day out there.' Martin says. 'You've been missing some great weather.'

His words are foolish. He goes to stand by the window and looks out at a single magpie stalking around the lawn.

'I want to tell you some things. Come and sit down. Yes, yes, yes, yes, yes, yes, yes.'

Martin sits like a dutiful son.

'I've come to a decision. It was like a bolt from the blue, you see.'

His words are slurred and difficult to understand. Martin wonders what time they're in now.

'Bolt from the blue, don't you know.'

'What was, Frank?'

He feels like a confessor, a therapist, a priest.

'You were. You were the bolt from the blue. I had no idea who you were, you see. No idea.'

'Who am I?'

He's gone too far. Frank is turning his head to one side, muttering. Just let him talk away, that's what Juliet had said. Just sit with him.

'Yes, yes, yes, yes yes.'

Martin looks at Frank's right hand, jittering on the bed covers.

He takes it in his own and smoothes the skin down. It's gnarled and rough, like the bark of an old tree, the lines like bark rings. He turns the palm over in his hands and circles the circumference with his thumb, traces down the lifeline. A long life, anyway. Over seventy's not bad – a good innings, Frank would say. The fingers close over his and he can feel the faint ticking of a heartbeat in the wrist.

'You've been good to me.'

Martin's surprised by the voice, looks up at the glassy eyes and, for a moment, sees Frank in them.

'I'm sorry I said those things yesterday. I didn't mean them. It was the heat of the moment. I was angry.'

'That's all right . . . Frank.'

He nearly said Dad. He feels the need to reassure, offer forgiveness – again the priest. The pressure on his hand intensifies as Frank leans forward awkwardly, his warped mouth hissing at him.

'I've decided not to take it. I'm giving it back. You take it.'

Martin tries to loosen the fierce grip a little.

'You take it!'

It's hurting.

'Okay, okay.'

The fingers relax again and Frank's head drops back on the pillow, his mouth sagging in disapproval.

'Yes, yes, yes, yes, yes.'

'Yes, Frank, it's okay.'

Martin withdraws his hand and sits back in his chair. Frank is murmuring.

'Thank you, Con.'

Connie now, is it? Martin sighs and rubs his wrist. He wishes Connie would hurry up. She shouldn't have left him alone with him. It's as if she blames him for all this.

Frank has relaxed now, his eyes closed again. Martin checks his watch: 10.45. He sits and looks at his hands, large hands, long fingers. He's always liked his fingernails, the way they curve pinkly; he can tell how healthy he is just by looking at the pallor of his nails. He strokes his forefinger down each nail on his left hand, is gratified by the smoothness. Martin wonders if his hands will ever look like Frank's do now, knotted and rough, like leather gardening gloves left outside until they curl and warp.

Frank's sleeping. He could go now – except that Connie will come and find him not there, the one thing she's asked him to do. He looks around the plain white room – a small ensuite, patterned print on the wall, the same yellow as the curtains – it reminds Martin of a small hotel room. He wonders how much it costs a night. Frank's bedside table is crowded, the only clutter in the room. There are the flowers, two glasses and a jug of water, two bottles of pills, a pile of unread magazines, a wet facecloth, a scattering of get well cards, and a manila folder with papers in it.

Martin picks up the folder and reads **Frank Finnigan, CVA 08, 29/1/98**. He opens it and finds an array of medical records, most of which consist of abbreviations and figures he doesn't understand, alongside indecipherable doctor scribble. Opthalmodynamometry. What the hell's that? Some brain scans are in the back of the folder. Martin holds the slippery clear film up to the light and watches Frank's brain light up. It's about the size of his fist, a convoluted wiring system curled into a strange flower. He wonders where the thalamus is, what it should look like, which cells have been killed off with lack of blood. He stares at it until his arm hurts with the effort of holding it up.

Among this mass of wrinkled organ are the building blocks from which Frank has built his world, all his different lives. Buried in these tiny twists and turns are the tales that give meaning to his day-to-day life. Here in his hand, Martin is looking at the ferment of genius: he is holding Frank's memories, his inner life. He feels an extraordinary fear at the thought. If Frank amounts to this pile of neurons, what happens when they die? Who is this man lying in front of him? Is he still Frank? He puts the folder back on the table and pours himself a glass of water. The room is hot and airless.

Frank opens his eyes, clear blue, and looks directly at Martin.

'I can't take it. You must keep it. You wrote it,' he says in a younger man's voice.

He can see me, thinks Martin.

As they sit looking at one another, Martin hears the door open behind him and turns to see in the doorway Connie and a man about his own age, a younger version of Frank but with Connie's jawline. He's surprised when the man greets him by name, Connie's disapproval fresh on his tongue.

'Martin.'

'Ian,' he replies.

Martin's finding it hard to get up in the mornings. He lies spread out across the double bed he once shared with Alice, and misses her presence, her laugh, her cuddling up against his back as they fall asleep, her cold feet warming themselves against his. He used to hate those cold feet. He lies looking at the ceiling, images of Alice or of Frank billowing across its whiteness, until he can stand it no longer and shuts his eyes against them, turns his face into the pillow, and soon his breathing deepens and he's dreaming again.

He wakes again a few hours later, but still will not get up. Instead he leans over and pulls a pen and paper out from the drawer of the bedside table and props himself up against the bedhead. He wants to write. His pen draws the outline of two perfect circles nestled together in a figure of eight, and goes over and over the shape until the paper is almost worn through. Then he writes.

I walk this winding road for miles
and soon it will be night.
I trip and fall and fear that I
may yet forsake this fight.
Midway upon this journey
I know not where I will
each signpost has a question
each turn another hill.
I dare not stop and sit awhile
I dare not ask you lest
you tell me you are lost as well
and I let go this quest.

When he's finished, Martin lies down and sleeps again. He's woken by the phone ringing but leaves it to the answerphone and goes to have a shower. The rest of the day seems to take an age. He doesn't feel like going out; he doesn't feel like working. He goes into his study once and takes out the manuscript of *The Game of the Few*. It's typewritten, with tiny spider-scribbled notes in the margins: it doesn't look like Frank's handwriting. He flicks through the pages but doesn't read, catching only a phrase or two in passing. He will have to go over it meticulously later, compare it with the handwritten editing and then the final version. He doesn't have the energy now. He tucks it back inside the box and closes it, leaves it sitting in the middle of the desk, like a precious egg incubating.

He goes to make himself lunch and notes there isn't much left in the fridge. He'll have to venture out sooner or later. He calculates the food will last until Wednesday or Thursday, if he's careful.

The phone is ringing again. Martin goes out into the hallway and listens to the answerphone message click on. It's the publisher: 'Hi Martin. Andrea Craig here, just checking up on how you're getting on. We heard that Frank's in hospital and were wondering . . . well, how he is really. I also wanted to check how you were getting on with the biography. We'd like to take a look at your first draft whenever it's ready. Give me a ring and we can discuss the situation. Great. Hope to hear from you soon.'

Martin presses the play button and listens to the previous message. It's Alice, wanting to know when she can bring Lance around. He dials her number absent-mindedly but when she picks up he panics and replaces the receiver. Not yet. He can't talk to her. He can't talk to anyone . . . Unless. No, he can't ring them. He'll wait until Frank's out of hospital, then maybe Ian will answer the phone and it'll look like he's just ringing to check on Frank. He goes into the lounge instead and switches on the television. Daytime soaps. Hoorah. He watches them blankly for a while, curled up on the couch. His eyes are sore. He closes them.

Martin wakes to the shrill ring of the telephone over the noise of the television news. It's twilight. He stumbles over the furniture to the hallway, rubbing his eyes, and picks up the phone through habit.

'Hello?'

'Hello, Martin. It's Ian Finnigan. We met the other day.'

Ian's ringing him? Martin shakes his head a little and straightens up, tries to concentrate.

'Yes, hello. How's Frank?'

'That's what I'm ringing about. He's had another stroke, I'm afraid. The doctors say this one is massive. He's not expected to pull through.'

Martin sits in his car in the hospital carpark. The sun is bright through the windscreen, its warmth soothing on his skin. He closes his eyes. It reminds him of his mother cupping his face with warm hands when he was a little boy in bed with a headache. Eventually a cloud passes over and the heat drops away. He opens his eyes. 2.41.

He gets out of the car and drags himself towards the entrance, then realises he's forgotten to lock the car and goes back. He stands at the driver's door a moment, imagining himself getting in and driving away, before sliding the key in the lock and turning it gently. He walks back to the entrance again. Inside there is that faint smell of lavender again. He breathes shallowly, trying not to take it in, and walks towards the lifts, one step at a time.

At the lift a woman in a wheelchair sits, waiting. She's younger than Martin, the skin on her face still tight and rosy. He wonders what's wrong with her, looks at her legs for clues, but she looks as if she has just sat down for a minute, her jeans bent at the knee, relaxed. He smiles at her, then feels a sudden fear she may speak to him and turns to press the lift button which is already lit.

They travel silently together, and Martin gets out at level two and goes to reception. He stands in front of the counter, waiting to check the room number with someone, procrastinating. The nurse at reception is busy. He waits patiently, watching her. He hasn't seen her before. She's solidly built, like a farm girl – she has those thick calves distinctive to New Zealanders. Martin watches her bend down to reach a file in the bottom drawer and wonders what she'd be like in bed, then is shocked by the thought. He hasn't had sex in a long while. Too long. Does Alice miss it too? Maybe Alice has already found someone else. John. He is angry at the thought and interrupts the nurse.

'Excuse me, can you tell me where to find Frank Finnigan?'

She looks up, strands of dark brown hair falling across her face. 'Who?'

'Frank Finnigan. He was in this ward last week.'

He watches her finger trace down the list of names, then again.

'No. Not here. Just a sec.' She calls out to the office behind. 'Maureen, do you know any Frank Finnigan?'

Another nurse comes out, looks at Martin, smiles in what he thinks could be a pitying way.

'He's been moved, love. Ward 16.'

The farm girl turns back to Martin and repeats the words as if he hadn't heard.

'Ward 16.'

'Thank you.'

He turns uncertainly, then looks back.

'Is Juliet around?'

'Juliet? No, it's her day off.'

'Oh.'

Martin walks quietly back to the lift and stands waiting for it to arrive. He thinks of green-eyed Juliet, wonders if she was with Frank when it happened, if anyone was with him. Would he have known what was happening? Is he still able to speak? Perhaps the other side has been affected. But he won't die. Not yet. Martin knows he won't. He realises the open lift doors are closing again and presses the button, too late.

The next time they open he gets in and presses level four. There are two doctors in the lift already, talking of some complicated surgical procedure. They talk as if there is no patient involved, no actual human being operated on. Martin releases his breath when they get out at level three. The next level up, the doors slide across with a whoosh of air, and he sees the other lifts across the passage. He doesn't get out, waits until the doors close again, and presses the ground-floor button, steadying himself with a hand on the rail, concentrating on his breathing.

It's all right. Everything's going to be all right.

Martin gets out at the ground floor and walks back to the carpark, counting breaths until he reaches his car. His keys fumble and drop, and as he reaches down to pick them up he feels dizzy; his vision spins to black. It may be a minute or less, it may be an hour later, he picks up his keys and gets in the car, sits there, hands on the wheel.

Frank.

Chapter 9

'You will only find the truth you are willing to see.'

Martin won't answer the phone. He has a superstition that if he does it will be bad news. He even avoids looking at it, skirts around the far side of the hallway when he has to pass it. Nevertheless, it's not long before the bad news comes. The day after the hospital visit, the third ring of the morning. Martin is coming down the stairs and stops, sits, listens to Connie's voice being recorded on the answerphone, echoing conspiratorially in his empty hallway. Her voice cracks like she's been hit.

'Just letting you know Frank has died.'

Not 'passed away', not 'departed', not even 'gone'. Died. Frank has died.

Martin swallows hard.

'They say it was for the best, a relief. The funeral will be on Friday, at St Mary of the Angels, 1 pm. I would like you to come, Martin.'

He doesn't take in the words. He remembers the image of Connie leaning over the hospital bed, Frank's contorted face.

Frank is dead.

Martin holds his head in his hands, a little spinning planet, and stares at the grey carpet. What will become of his work? What will become of him? The strength of the feeling rocks him. Only an old man, a cantankerous old bugger, remember. But it's hard to remember, hard to picture Frank now. Only that weakened, frail man in hospital comes to mind.

Martin gets to his feet, goes to have a shower. It's too hot, yet he doesn't turn it down, stands in the steam, feeling the hot pellets of water sting his skin, raise little red marks. He feels faint, puts one hand against the damp wall to support himself. If only he had finished the book. The publishers will want it double quick now, that's for sure. Martin puts his face under the stream of hot water, feels it against his cheeks, like burning tears. He gets out quickly, dries himself, noticing the line and length of his limbs, the feel of the towel as it rasps over his shoulders. He puts a finger to the steamed-over mirror and traces the outline of his face, wipes away the fog within to look at himself – the thinning hair, watery eyes, sharp jaw. There are traces of grey at his temples.

Later, lying on his bed, naked, Martin wonders what he feels. People talk of loss, and yet this is not an emptiness, not an absence. Rather he feels he has gained something, an extra layer, a coarse hardness silting around his heart and solidifying. A heavy weight is growing inside him. He imagines it there; wonders if other people might be able to see it, pulsing in his chest. He closes his eyes.

'How'd you be?'

Frank's voice. Even if he can't remember his face clearly, he still has his voice.

Martin gets dressed and goes down to the study, rummages through some tapes and selects one. Reminds himself he must send those photos off to Te Papa for the exhibition. He sits at his desk and places the tape recorder on the ink blotter, presses play. And there, there is Frank, sitting back in his battered leather chair, his eyebrows twitching, his fist thumping the desk:

'Well of course he didn't. The man's a bloody fool. Anyone can see that.'

'That's a bit harsh. He's very well thought of in the English Department and his wife is a very respected editor.'

'Contradiction in terms, old chap. Just look at his introduction in that latest anthology, feting Adair for writing such bullshit.'

'You weren't in that anthology were you?'

'Now look, Martin. This isn't professional jealousy. The man's a prig. Always turns up to my book launches, although I certainly never invite him and he knows I don't like him. Swans around, hobnobbing, drinking all the booze and earbashing anyone who will listen about his latest project. Talking about the "irrelevance of popularity". How can a bloody writer talk about popularity being irrelevant. That's what pays the fucking bills! Even to look at him you can tell he's got no brains. His eyes are too near the top of his head.'

Martin smells the pipe smoke drift through his study.

'What do you think about being a popular writer?'

'I think it's bloody brilliant.'

'I mean, what do you think about the way some people downgrade populist writing?'

'Well, there's a difference between popular and populist for a start. I would say I was one of the former. It's not that I work at that, you know, or even aim to produce bestsellers, I never imagine myself writing for the bloody airport bookshops. I guess, in the early days before the success, I always wanted my work to be popular . . . but as it was, not to have to change to be popular.'

'When you look back on those early days and you look at the early work, what's your reaction to it?'

'Some of it's Godawful. You know that, you've read it. It felt dreadful. At one time I was going to give up . . . or I thought I wanted to give up. But Connie wouldn't support that. She sat me down at my typewriter, told me I wouldn't get any dinner until I'd written three pages and left me to it. I never wrote to be fucking popular, you know. I didn't even write to make money really, but that happened to be a requirement, to provide for my family. I was never enough of an artist to let the children go unclothed or unfed. But it was a big risk, leaving journalism, leaving all prospects of a stable income. "You realise, Mr Finnigan", said the news editor when I resigned, "you realise that while writing fiction is the cream in your coffee, journalism is your bread and butter". Hah. And I said I hope to have a lot more cream in my coffee in the near future.'

'Is it an occupation of compulsion?'

'If life doesn't constantly interrupt.'

Connie is calling something out in the background.

'There it is interrupting now.'

And that glorious guffaw, that burst of sound, that essence of Frank. Martin feels the pressure in his chest tighten, a weight like a stone carried within him, a new and heavy knowledge.

The day of the funeral is overcast. 'A bull's backside day', Frank would have called it. Funny how so many of his metaphors were rural, yet he'd never lived on a farm. You must simply pick up those things growing up in provincial New Zealand, Martin thinks, as he puts his tie on in front of the mirror. He has trouble with the knot, his fingers are numb, unable to grasp the material firmly. Perhaps he's dressing too formally. Frank would have laughed at him. But then, Frank would have loved the whole thing: friends, family, peers. Bloody hypocrites, he would have grumped. Martin smiles weakly at himself in the mirror, puts on his jacket. All set.

The car won't start. Martin continues to turn the key, listens to the coughing engine jigger and die twelve times over. Fucking thing! He hits the steering wheel hard with the base of his hand, hits it again in pain. He checks the petrol: quarter full, should be fine. Must be the bastard battery, must've left the front door ajar or something, ran it down from the door light. He turns the key again, almost twisting the metal. He'll have to take a cab. Or walk – yeah, walk. It's not that far, he'd have trouble parking anyway. He slams the garage door and strides down the street.

It starts to spit. A bull-bum day. Martin watches his feet,

consciously directing them forward, left, right. Bloody fucking car. He walks past a new townhouse development, avoids the builder's growling dog, turns down the top of Kelburn Parade and checks his watch. Plenty of time, no worries, left, right, left.

By the time he reaches the Allenby Terrace steps it's raining properly. Martin takes the steps two at a time, feeling the wetness clamp his hair to his forehead. There are other people outside the church, hurrying towards the doors, he's not the only one wet. He glances up at the spire, glimpses a white Madonna in flowing robes, her hands outstretched towards him in sympathy. He imagines she looks down, down, directly to his heart, sees the hungry troll sitting there, clutching it.

Martin selects a pew towards the back. Those further up are mostly full anyway; the church is packed. He can see the family up the front, Connie in a navy blue twinset – why had he expected her in a melodramatic veil?; Ian in a black suit on her right; and a woman who must be the daughter, the frizzy hair of Frank, but black not grey, her face turned away from him. Perhaps that was the granddaughter who handed him the service pamphlet at the door? Her young eyes had a hint of Frank behind them, dulled with the seriousness of the occasion. Martin looks at the pamphlet. There's a photo of Frank on the front. Francis John Finnigan, 6/1/27–20/2/98. That huge moustache like a large moth about to take flight, those bristling eyebrows, the piercing eyes.

Stupid old bastard.

Martin blinks his eyes in anger.

He looks up at the ceiling, concentrates on the stained-glass windows far above the arches. He can't make them out. The large window above the altar is of Christ, of course, hanging forlorn on the cross with women weeping at his bloody feet. The lower side windows on his right are of Joan of Arc, Peter Chanel. He looks across to the opposite windows of Our Lady of Christ, St Francis Xavier, and sees a man kneeling on the bar, clutching rosary beads. They are bright egg-blue. The sight shocks Martin.

It hasn't registered that Frank is Catholic. They've held conversations about religion, and Frank has said his parents were Catholic. Coming from such a large family, what else could his father be? But he'd been brought up atheist, or maybe agnostic – 'faithless', Frank said. What is he doing at the end of his life being farewelled in this great Catholic church with its swinging balls of incense and icons ringing the walls? Perhaps it's Connie's doing. Martin looks up the aisle to her, but someone is standing between them, shaking her hand. He sees Ian beside her, the dutiful son, one hand on an elbow. You can almost tell by the way he's standing Ian's gay. Martin realises he never raised the issue with Frank. He can imagine the eruption it would have caused. Martin's eyes drift upwards to the figure of Christ, impaled on the cross.

He shuffles along as two women enter the pew next to him. Perhaps they are fellow writers, or relations, or maybe just fans. There are hundreds of people in the church now. Martin looks around and recognises some: people he's interviewed, the odd celebrity. The Arts and Culture Minister – now that's ironic. Elena. Sid Hewlitt. Dame Harriet Wallace and Sarah Tandy. Jimmy Sullivan. Brett Healey. That couldn't be Daphne Withers, could it? Frank would be astounded to see her here, she's a notorious recluse. 'Wouldn't go out to a dogtucker's picnic,' says Frank.

For such a large crowd, people are very quiet and still, whispering, shuffling respectfully. Martin finds it creepy. He's glad when the service proper begins.

The priest is older than Frank; his voice creaks like a tree in wind. Martin lets the words waft over him. It's not until the congregation stands to sing the first hymn that he notices the coffin up the front, by the altar. It's large and black; it looks closed. Frank would have wanted it closed. *I don't want all those buggers peering in at me, checking that I'm really dead. Let them wonder about it.* He must be in there, though. Frank must be lying in that long, black box. Martin's eyes are watering. He turns them to the ceiling with its high wooden struts and arches. It looks like the upturned hull of a Viking ship. They are all floating along in it, upside down.

The priest is calling on someone else to speak. Joseph Levy. He looks older too since Martin saw him last, nearly a year ago. They have to adjust the microphone, and it squawks rudely.

'I've known Frank Finnigan for more than forty years. We first met in Wellington Hospital on the day our first children were born, the first of May 1958. My wife and I had a little girl, Jane, and Frank and Connie also had a little girl, Nancy. In those days men weren't encouraged in the delivery room and Frank and I were pacing up and down the waiting room together for some hours. Frank was telling tales, some of which I later found out weren't entirely true, but all of which were extremely amusing and which served to pass the anxious time very well. After the births we met up for a drink in a nearby pub and ever since have been the best of friends.'

He pauses and Martin sees a flick of paper, realises he's reading from notes.

'That's how I remember Frank, a teller of tales. And that's how many people throughout the world, people who never met the man, will remember him: for his books. His wit and irony, his perceptive observation of those he met in everyday life, his hopes and fears, his vision for the future – all remain very much alive in his writing.

'For those who never met Frank Finnigan, the man you sense behind the words in his stories and novels is fairly true to life. But there was so much more to the life. He was indeed one of those people who can be described as "larger than life". Everything Frank did was large, loud, significant. Even in his quiet, reflective moments there was a sense of importance in his words. His words were not always so well chosen – they could be harsh and cruel at times – but Frank was not a harsh, cruel man. He simply said what he thought, believing people would value the truth more than they would resent the bluntness. And in the end people usually did.

'That didn't mean he could always accept such bluntness in others. He was particularly sensitive to criticism of his work, and for some years refused to read reviews, as they invariably made him livid. However, he could not resist for long and I remember him relating to me with great satisfaction an occasion when he had actually gone down to a newspaper office and demanded to speak to the reviewer. Fortunately no physical violence ensued; in fact, the two ended up going out to lunch together and spent the rest of the afternoon vigorously engaged in a discussion about the merits of various books. Frank loved being loved. And we all loved loving him.'

Joseph hesitates, his eyes on the lectern, then turns to one side, his mouth tight, and walks quickly back to his seat. Martin senses his speech was only half through. They stand for 'Amazing Grace'.

Frank loved being loved. That's true. The need to be loved was certainly a prime motivation of his characters. *To save a wretch like me.*

Did he love Frank? Martin raises his eyes to the battened ceiling and searches his relationship with Frank. Yes, he finds love; and also hate, pity, shame, impatience, fear, all these things within himself. How had he described it to Alice at the beginning? 'An affinity.' Alice is right. Writing a biography is like falling in love. You see a greatness, a uniqueness, a special peculiarity in a life, and hunger for it. You hunger for something ideal, and find in the end something flawed. It is hubris to suppose the whole truth is given, or able to be. His eyes blur as the congregation sits at the end of the hymn. The priest is speaking again.

'It is always fitting for people who have known the deceased well to speak at the funeral, to give a fuller picture of the life. Thank you, Mr Levy, for sharing some of your memories with us today. I myself only met Mr Finnigan a few weeks ago, when he was first admitted to hospital. He was no longer the man he had been, but I found a good man, a man who was afraid, a man seeking healing and forgiveness. As life draws to an end, people often fear the loss of power, control; but with acceptance comes a positivity and a new wisdom. I believe Frank Finnigan was reaching towards that. Now I would like to ask his son Ian Finnigan to say a few words.'

The priest visited him in hospital? Perhaps Connie had asked him. It seems unlikely that Frank would have, even if he had thought he was dying, and he'd given every indication of denying that. Martin tries to imagine the priest at his bedside, Frank clasping his hand, asking for forgiveness. The image doesn't ring true.

Ian's voice brings his focus back to the lectern. He even sounds like Frank, but with a lighter tone, a slight Australian accent. He's talking of when he was a child.

'My father would take me out hunting occasionally with a couple of his mates. I loved the camping trips, staying in tents in the woods, washing in the rivers, but I hated the guns. I wouldn't go near them, hated it whenever they made a kill, which fortunately wasn't very often. But when they did get something, Dad would make me go up to the dying animal, deer or pig, whatever, and finish it off. I could never quite measure up.' He smiles sadly at his sister Nancy in the front row. 'We never really understood each other.'

Martin recalls Frank's words which he took for jest at the time: 'I often wonder if he can really be my son.' He remembers Frank mistaking him for Ian at the hospital, talking to him as a father.

'Frank would want me to say what I mean. There was nothing he hated worse than a hypocrite. So I'm going to. Frank, you were a bloody useless father. You taught me to fear you. You taught me I could never be good enough.'

Martin's hands shake with rage. How dare he, at his own father's funeral?

'But I understand now that you taught me only what you had been taught. I want to tell you two things, Dad. And now, at last, you have to listen. I want to tell you, I love you. I want to tell you, you were good enough. And so am I. Goodbye Frank. Goodbye Dad.'

Frank would hate this.

Martin feels very alone.

Elena sees Martin outside the church. She looks very elegant in a short black dress, white gloves, white hat and shoes. Her eyeliner is slightly smudged.

'Martin.'

He loves the way she says his name. Like a cognac.

'Always nice to see you, Elena.'

She brings out the gentleman in him.

'Would you like a lift to the cemetery?'

'Please.'

'We can be the outcasts travelling together.'

He wonders why she thinks of him as a fellow outcast. Elena smiles at him conspiratorially and leads the way to her car. A Daimler, would you believe. The leather seats smell of cigars, old memories.

'Did you like the service?'

'Yes, I thought it lovely. Frank would have liked to see all those people there. And you, what did you think, Mr Biographer? Will it make a fitting final chapter?'

Martin shivers. 'That's crass. Did you see him before he died, in hospital? I saw him, his disintegration. I will write none of that. It's humiliating. I won't do that to Frank.'

He's surprised by his own vehemence.

Elena eyes him briefly without turning her head.

'What will you do to him, I wonder?'

'We will see, won't we.'

He deliberately looks to the left, watching a blur of houses flit past. They turn up Makara hill.

'It's such a shame that Frank will not read it, don't you think? But perhaps it will be a better book for it.'

Martin doesn't want to know what she means. He wishes he'd never accepted the lift. They reach a stream of cars heading to the cemetery, slow as an ant march, trooping over the hill. Houses fade to gorse and broom, patches of wild orange and yellow bristling on the hillsides. It's starting to rain again.

'So what did you think of the service anyway, Martin?'

'Most of it was fine. But his son's speech I thought was appalling. Very inappropriate. It did no justice to Frank's qualities as a father at all.'

'Surely he would know Frank's qualities as a father better than anyone. Have you met Ian before?'

'No, not really. But I don't imagine I would gain much from it, judging from that speech.'

'You may be surprised. But then you don't like to be surprised, do you, Martin?'

'What do you mean?'

'I mean you seem to do all you can to avoid being surprised.'

'If you mean I do thorough research, yes, I do. I know you didn't like the way I asked about your relationship with Frank. You may view it as prying, but I view it as research.'

They crawl past a concrete wall smeared with graffiti at the top of the hill. The hills beyond are flecked with sheep and baby pine trees.

'And what is all this "research" for? What are you aiming to find?'

'The truth. The truth of Frank's life.'

'Ah well. That would be something. But you will only get the truth people choose to give you, you know. And you will only find the truth you are willing to see.'

They are silent for the rest of the journey. The rain stops as the Daimler motors up the driveway. Welcome to Makara Cemetery. The stream of cars turns left and trickles towards the main grounds. Assyrians, Serbian Orthodox, Muslim, Tung Jung, Poon Fah, Interdenominational and right again, down to the Roman Catholics. Elena and Martin get out of the car and head across the wet grass to the graveside. Only a quarter of those from the church are here. Martin hangs back, on the edge of the group. He watches the pallbearers lift the coffin from the hearse and carry it over to the grave, place it on the straps to be slowly lowered in.

Frank.

Martin thinks of what he said to Elena, that he's looking to find the truth of Frank's life. In the beginning he was. In the beginning he was obsessed with it. But now he's not so sure. It seems such an impossible thing. There are so many different versions, so many different 'truths'. It is more the meaning of his life he's reaching for. He was on the edge of it just when Frank died. Now he can no longer help him.

The priest is intoning Latin prayers over the coffin; the group of people are huddled together around the hole in the wet ground. Martin feels out of place. Elena's right. He is an outsider, like her, though Frank feels more like one of his family than his own parents do. Yet here he's shut out. There's no one he can turn to.

Despair seeps through the weight in his heart and cracks it open like an egg.

At the wake, Martin stands on the edges of small groups of people, nibbling at sandwiches. They talk of Frank. Some of the stories he hasn't heard before and could make useful anecdotes for the book, but he can't be bothered making notes, and knows he won't remember them afterwards. Someone's talking about the exhibition on Frank that's going to be shown at the museum. He still hasn't sent off those photos they wanted.

'You're the biographer.'

'Yes. That's right.'

'Oh it's so lucky you began before he died. It'll be like a tribute to him. When is it due out?'

It's strange being back in the house again, with no Frank. He goes to the toilet, and on his way back to the lounge passes the stairway to the study, hesitates, then softly steps on to the stairs and creeps down into the room.

It's dark in the study, a curtain is pulled halfway across the french doors. But otherwise it seems much as Frank would have left it. Martin sits down in his usual hard chair opposite the desk and imagines Frank propped in his leather throne, explaining why he's right about something and everyone else is wrong. But Frank doesn't come. Instead he hears a step on the stair and looks up to see Ian in the room.

'Escaping the throng? Can't stand wakes myself.' He smiles, takes a seat in the leather chair and settles back comfortably, too comfortably. 'I suppose you'll want to interview me some time.'

Martin doesn't reply.

'Or do I not fit? An ungrateful effeminate son who ran off to Australia never to be seen again. I don't know, sounds a good story to me.'

'It doesn't sound like one of Frank's stories.'

'No, it needs a more exciting ending. Perhaps you could make out that I killed him.'

Martin wonders what shows in his face.

'Aren't you going to ask me what he was like as a father?'

'I think you made your views very clear in the speech at the funeral.'

'You didn't like it?'

'No.'

'How did I know you were going to say that. What do you do

for a living, Martin? Are you a full-time writer? Sorry if I'm supposed to know, but I'm out of touch with this country.'

'I'm an academic.'

'Ah. Really? I wouldn't have thought Dad would let an academic anywhere near his biography.'

'He asked me to do it.'

'You surprise me more. You must have special qualities.'

Martin wishes Ian wasn't sitting in his father's chair.

'Well what would you like to know about dear old Daddy?'

'Surely you could save the disrespect for today? The day of his funeral.'

'Why should I? He never saved his disrespect. He was quite open in his scorn of me and the way I live. He was a vicious, frightened old man, and I'm not going to pretend otherwise.'

'Did he not come to accept you?'

'He never accepted me, not since I came out as a teenager. Didn't tell you about that though, did he? Doesn't want the world to know his only son's a poof.'

'Connie told me.'

'I'm not surprised. She loves me at least. But I disgusted him.'

'You sound proud of it.'

'I'm not ashamed of it, not anymore. I used to be ashamed, ashamed of hating him. Then I realised, there was no point even trying. I gave up being someone else and became me. My mother's love was enough.'

'You had Frank's love as well.'

'You're very defensive of him.'

'Perhaps I'm thinking of my own son. It's not easy being a father, you know.'

'Want some free advice? Be there.'

Martin blinks at him and Ian looks contrite.

'I better get back up there. Do the dutiful son thing.'

He laughs and goes back up the stairs. Martin exhales, closes his eyes. What did you think of that, Frank? But Frank's not there.

He gets up from the chair, takes a last look around the room and follows Ian up the stairs. He needs to go home.

Connie's in the kitchen, pouring boiling water into a huge teapot.

'You should let someone else do that.'

'I don't mind. It's good to keep busy.' She puts the teapot down on the bench and looks at him. 'That's good advice, Martin.'

'What?' He's thinking of what Ian said.

'Keeping busy. You should get back on to that book.'

How did she know he hadn't been working on it?

'You're right. I should. I will.'

'Good. I'm looking forward to reading it. Would you like a cup of tea?'

'No, I have to go, Connie.' He puts his hands on her shoulders. 'I'm sorry.'

He's not entirely sure what he is apologising for. 'I'm sorry too.'

They hug awkwardly as someone comes into the kitchen.

'Shall I make more tea, Connie? Oh, you have already.'

'All under control, Bea, all under control. We'll see you again some time then, Martin.'

'I'll bring the manuscript round when it's done.'

When it's done, he thinks as he walks up the garden path. The bloody thing will never be done.

Martin's buttering his breakfast toast when he feels someone in the room with him. He turns slowly. It's Alice.

'What the hell are you doing here?'

'I live here, or have you forgotten?'

'Sorry, it's just you gave me a hell of a fright. I wasn't expecting you.'

He looks down at the buttery knife held out menacingly and

feels foolish. They laugh. The first time they've laughed in ages.

'Want some toast?'

'Yes, please.'

'So.' He puts more bread in the toaster. 'You live here, do you?' He's scared of what she'll say. Alice looks wary.

'We have to talk about that.'

Martin's lightness grows heavy again. He makes a fresh plunger of coffee, hands Alice her toast and sits at the table with her, watching her slim hands deftly slide butter across the pieces. She has beautiful hands. He notices she's still wearing her wedding ring.

'Where's Lance?'

'With Mum.'

They sip and chew together. Martin remembers how the sound of her chewing used to annoy him, especially when he was reading. Now he listens to it with something like nostalgia.

'Are you all right?'

He's startled by her voice.

'Yes, yes, just thinking.'

'No, I mean are you all right in general? Since Frank . . .'

'. . . died.'

'Yes.'

'Yes.'

He looks down gloomily at the tablecloth, finishes his coffee. He doesn't know what to say to her – perhaps something about Lance; looks up to try and is amazed to see tears on her face.

'Alice. Alice. It's all right. I'm all right. Really. What's wrong?'

'What's wrong? Jesus, Martin. What do you want me to do? Do you want me and Lance to stay away? Do you want a divorce? I need to know what's going to happen now.'

'I don't know. How the hell do I know?'

Martin gets up and paces around the room, angry at the helplessness.

'I thought it was you who knew what would happen. You

seemed to have it all planned out so far. What do you want?'

'You.'

Alice's voice is small and quiet. He will not be manipulated like this.

'Well you had me. And you ran away. So there you go.'

It's so unfair of her to come here like this, pretend it was all down to him. He's had nothing to do with it, as far as he can see – not with the decisions anyway. She decided to leave, she decided to take Lance away. Little Lance, kicking a soccer ball around the yard, laughing at the strangest things, coming into his study all the time, wanting something. He should have paid more attention. Martin feels faint, sits down again, head in his hands. He feels Alice stroking his hair. She used to do that when they were young and he was studying, sneak up on him and stroke his hair until he looked up.

'I love you, Martin. And I want to be with you. But you were making it impossible. You were obsessed. It was like living with someone else. It was like living with Frank.'

He looks up, almost spits. 'How do you know who Frank was? You never even met him.'

'I may not have met him, but I knew him all right. You were becoming more and more like him. You didn't even realise it, did you? You started talking like him; you were always quoting him; you bought clothes like him. Remember that hat? God knows you never bought a hat in your life. It wouldn't have been long before you bought a bloody pipe.'

'Don't be ridiculous.'

'It was ridiculous. It was ridiculous that you didn't see what was happening. Together the two of you were so absorbed in your own self-importance, your own needs, you ignored the rest of us, the people who love you.'

'If you loved me so much, you would have been here when I needed you.'

Alice sighs. 'Martin.'

He clenches and unclenches his hands under the table.

'Well, he's gone now,' he says. 'Dead and gone. So he won't worry you anymore. You and Lance can come back.'

'But is he really gone?'

He feels his eyes fill and overflow, the tickle of water as it creeps down his face, the taste of salt on his lips. Alice has her arms around him, is rocking him like a baby, but the tears won't stop. He cries for Frank. And he cries for Alice and Lance. He cries for himself. Slivers of the heavy stone inside break off and crumble, dissolve into him and are cried out. His chest heaves with the effort.

At the end of it Martin's exhausted, an empty shell. Alice takes him by the hands and leads him upstairs, tucks him up into bed. He's incapable of resisting. He feels her hand on his forehead, stroking back his damp hair. It is soft and cool.

In his study, Martin finds a note on his desk in Alice's clear hand: Tomorrow I'll send Lance to stay with you for a while. I'll come back when you've finished the book. Love Alice.

He reads it again, props it up against his card catalogue. Thank you. Better get to work then.

Martin sits at his chair and empties the last box from Frank out on the desk. He sorts the letters into order by date, and cross-references them in his catalogue. He has most of them already but a few are new discoveries: two letters from an old school friend living in England in the early '60s and one reply by Frank. The short story drafts are definitely new and valuable additions. Dated August and September 1979 they must have been written just after the *Plums* collection was published and were omitted from the next collection, *The Stories of Frank Finnigan*, in 1991. He could print them in full in the biography: they are good examples of his style at the time – the interest in the constricting effects of a materialistic society and attempts by the characters to escape from it.

Lastly he picks up the manuscript of *The Game of the Few* and weighs it in his hands carefully, like a new-born child. This, this is the real gift. This is what he's been waiting for. Perhaps the last pieces of the puzzle lie within these pages. Martin takes a pen and paper and the manuscript with him into the lounge and settles down in the large armchair.

The virgin story engrosses him as fully as it did on his first reading of the published bestseller. It's different, though, an entirely new flavour: it surprises Martin, it's so unlike the other first drafts of Frank's works. The others had not been reworked to this extent before publication. Even a different title. It excites him to see the scope for analysis, the revelation of the workings of the artist. So, this is how such a work comes about, how brilliance is born. Martin reads quickly, skimming the pages in his eagerness to devour the chapters. On each page he reads the faded red ink marks in the margins last, savouring their understanding after the original version has been swallowed. He can hardly believe his luck.

The ending comes too quickly. He is scarce up to the epilogue before he wants to start over, read it again with renewed knowledge. He makes himself read the final paragraphs slowly, tasting each word on his tongue, placing them delicately on lines in the air. The last coupling: THE END. And below, initials, a deliberate CF, 1/12/69.

Martin hears the last piece slot into place with a quiet click.

Chapter 10

'Are we even capable of understanding ourselves?'

Martin wakes to hear a knocking noise and for a moment has no idea where he is. He blinks the bedroom into focus and realises the sound above the thudding of his heart is someone tapping on the door. Confused, he calls for them to come in. A small barrel of a boy rockets towards the bed.

'Lance!'

'Mum dropped me off.'

Lance worms himself under the bedclothes, wriggles down the end to tickle Martin's feet, and is rewarded by a squeal.

'Right, that's it!'

They tussle amidst the sheets, bucking the duvet into sudden sea monsters and sending the quilt of blue oceans sliding to the floor.

'Truce!'

The pair lie back exhausted against the pillows. Martin looks at his son's slender wrists, gripped between his own wad of fingers. He watches the young, bony chest heaving for air, and smiles in delight at the perfect, small body.

'Hi, Dad.'

Lance nuzzles up to him with the complete lack of self-consciousness only children possess. It won't be long before that's gone. Martin wraps his huge arms around the boy and closes his eyes to stop the tears.

'What would you like to do today, then?'

The boy's words are muffled against Martin's chest. 'Go smimming.'

'Swimming, is it? All right then, go find some togs.' Martin slaps him on the backside as Lance swings his spindly legs over the side of the bed. 'No time to waste!'

The boy screeches out into the hallway and Martin stands in the middle of the room and stretches, arms up to the ceiling, yawning loudly. He feels as if he's been asleep a long time. Some exercise will do him good. He goes to take a shower, singing a little. The water is cold at first, then suddenly hot, and he yelps, grabs at the taps. His skin seems more sensitive today. Martin moves his face under the stream of water, feels the warm fingers pat his forehead, his eyes, and parts his lips to allow a drop or two to land on his tongue. He swallows, opens his mouth again to shout out to Alice asking where his togs are, and remembers, closes it again.

When he comes out, Lance is waiting impatiently on the stairs, jogging up and down.

'Aren't you ready yet?' Martin asks in a surprised tone.

'Dad!'

'Won't be long. Go make yourself a sandwich. And make me one while you're at it.'

Lance slides down the banister happily. By the time Martin comes down he's halfway through a bread roll smeared with peanut butter. He hands another stickily to Martin, grins at him. Martin tries not to pay attention to the feeling.

'Let's go then.'

Lance chatters away in the car, relating tales of who did what to whom at school on Friday afternoon, how he's going to enter the school triathlon and would Martin sponsor him, because it was for the school, and he had to do five laps of the pool, and bike right up the hill and back and then run for a kilometre. Martin lets his shoulders drop, erases all the lists written at the back of his eyes, hears the words as if they are a play script, registers them and lets them go, drives automatically, his mind a calm blankness.

At the pool he shepherds Lance into the men's changing rooms. His son. He's taking his son swimming. They get changed next to each other. Martin notices Lance glancing at his body. It won't be long before he's a man himself. He wishes he could delay it somehow, keep him as a child. It's noisy by the poolside. Everything echoes: kids shouting, splashing, ZMFM blaring in the background. The air smells of chlorine. Martin watches Lance paddling around the medium pool for a while, then goes to do a few lengths in the adult lanes.

Everything slows. He swims up the lane and back again, kicking strongly, feeling the muscles in his calves and thighs tighten and stretch, his arms reach out for the stroke, his breath held, then head turning for a gasp of air, his ribs rising and falling, the pull of his body through water. A single question runs through his head: what to do with his discovery. Now he can no longer deny the truth, what will he do with it? He sucks air into his lungs, holds it there with the question, gasps it back out again and gulps in more. Stroke, stroke, turn and breathe. His body aches with effort, yet he feels perfectly still.

After twenty laps he pauses by the side, looks up to see Lance sitting on a bench, towel wrapped around his skinny shoulders, shivering. He gets out and goes over to him.

'Sorry, did I take too long?'

''S all right.'

'Let's get you a hot drink.'

They get dressed and go to the cafe. Martin orders a hot chocolate for Lance and a latte for himself. They sit at a corner table and sip their drinks, not speaking for a while. A husband and wife are at the next table with their little boy; the woman is saying something to the man, and he smiles and takes her hand. Martin looks away.

'I'm glad you've come back home,' he says to Lance, who grins at him, a line of white froth rimming his upper lip. 'When do you think your mother will come back?'

Lance's smile slowly dissolves as he eyes his father. He takes a deliberate slurp of his hot chocolate, looking down at the table as he replies.

'When she's ready.'

Smart kid.

'Is that what she said to you?'

Lance looks up casually, his face unreadable. 'She said when you'd finished the book.'

Another slurp of hot chocolate.

'When are you going to finish the book anyway?'

Now there's a question.

'When I'm ready.'

Lance chokes a little on his drink and Martin feels ashamed. He rubs his back, offers him a serviette.

'I think I'm almost ready, Lance. I just have to talk to one more person and then finish the last chapter.'

The boy looks up at him, still coughing a little, his eyes watering.

'Mum says you found out a big secret.'

'Yes, I did.'

He shouldn't have told her, shouldn't have told anyone, not yet.

The boy seems to guess at his thoughts. 'Is it a secret you have to keep or one you can tell?'

'I'm not sure yet, Lance.'

He has the most beautiful smile.

'It'll be choice when you're finished, won't it, Dad?'

He smiles back.

'Yep. It'll be real choice.'

Instead of going home, Martin turns right and drives past the airport, up towards Frank's house.

'I just have to go see someone before we go home, Lance. Okay?'

'Okay.'

Martin parks the car just before the driveway, gets out and looks down into the garden. As well tended as ever: Connie's keeping busy then. He turns back to the car and knocks on the window.

'Want to come in?'

They go down the path together, Lance stepping neatly in the middle of each terracotta tile, avoiding the cracks. Martin represses the urge to tell him to behave himself and rings the bell. He hasn't been here since the wake. He closes his eyes briefly, sees Frank coming to the door, waving a newspaper angrily: *'If they took out all the crap, they could fit it on a bloody postage stamp!'*

But Connie is there, in a pale blue dress and her house slippers. Russian music is playing in the lounge.

'Martin, come in. Nice to see you. And this is your boy, is it? Hello, come in.'

'Yes, this is Lance. Sorry to just drop in on you like this.'

'That's all right. I quite miss it.' Her eyes twinkle.

She shows them into the lounge, turns the music down.

'Reminds me of home. Would you like a drink?'

'Not for me, thanks. Lance?'

'No, thank you.'

Didn't need to tell him to behave after all.

'And how old are you, Lance?'

'Eight. I'll be nine in June.'

'I have just the thing for you. Here, come look at this.'

She takes out a wooden model aeroplane from a cupboard behind the couch.

'My grandson couldn't finish this the other day. Do you think you could?'

'I might.'

Martin smiles at the boy's caution, watches them as they carry the plane carefully through to the next room and set it up on the dining table. Connie comes back and leaves the door ajar, sits closer to Martin.

'So, how are you getting on?'

God, she's expecting the manuscript.

'Oh, it's not quite finished yet.'

He pauses. How to say this?

'But that last box of stuff Frank left me has been remarkably useful.'

'Oh, yes.'

She can't have known.

'It included the original manuscript of *The Game of the Few*, which everyone thought had been lost.'

There is surprise: her sparse white eyebrows rise a little, the corner of her mouth twitches. Martin remembers how he used to revel in springing one of his discoveries on Frank; how he would choose the exact moment in the conversation to float it out on the air, and savour the effect as it batted into his nose, and watch his mouth and eye-bags dropping down into the face of a bloodhound. This is quite different. He wants Connie to somehow force it out of him. She is settling back in her chair.

'Was it very different from the published version?'

So, the game.

'Well, yes, it was. Not in the plot, that was much the same. But the style – it's difficult to explain – the style was rather more intellectual, more political. It was rather like the original had been translated.'

'And which do you think you enjoyed more?'

She is good at this, better than Frank. No bluster, just swift, unexpected returns.

'Enjoyed? Well, this may sound strange, but I believe I benefited more from reading the original after the final edition.'

'How so?'

She's leaning forward a little. The music in the background

makes her seem more European, more inscrutable. Martin thinks of the manuscript; knows he's out of his depth.

'If I had read the original first, I don't think I would understand it so well. I don't think I would understand Frank so well.'

'Why do you think he gave it to you?'

Her voice is full of wonder. She hadn't expected it, she's afraid.

'I don't know. Perhaps for the same reason you gave me his diaries.'

'Yes, I see.'

She's thoughtful. Martin sees it had been an impulse, and is curious.

'What prompted that? Why *did* you give me the diaries?'

Her smile is bashful, wry, as if she has been caught out.

'I'm not sure really. I think it was because we had been talking about Ian, about being brave enough to stand up for the truth. Frank had told me what he was doing the night before and I was so angry about it. More guilt, I suppose. Guilt compounding on guilt.'

Her vowels are clipped, the slightest trace of an accent. How could he not have made the connections before?

They look at each other as if they have never met.

'And what does this mean for your biography?'

Martin's hands ache and he looks down at them in bewilderment, expecting to see his wrists pulsing with purple blood. His words could be to himself.

'It means I don't understand anything at all.'

He daren't look up for fear she's smiling.

'To understand that is to understand something,' she says. She is not smiling. 'What are you going to do?'

'It is all beautifully ironic really, don't you think? If novels give us the illusion we understand others, biographies must surely take that one step further, into delusion. What do I know of Frank Finnigan? What did he know of me? Are we even capable of understanding ourselves?'

'Some of us progress further along that path than others.'

They are silent for a while.

'So what will you do?' she asks again, a note of fear.

'Perhaps I should be asking you that.'

Connie looks him straight in the eye. 'Many years ago, Martin, I performed an act of love. I will not betray that.'

'Not for an act of truth?'

'Truth? There are many kinds of truth, have you not found?'

'It rather blows my theory of biographical explication of art.'

He laughs, a bitter taste in the back of his throat, then notices Lance standing in the doorway and blinks.

'Finished?'

'Yes, look.'

They go and admire the patched up plane that surely would never fly.

'We better be going.'

At the front door, Connie takes a corner of his sleeve, her voice low.

'You still haven't told me what you will do.'

That night, after Martin has put Lance to bed, he sits in his study, rocking back and forth on the legs of his chair. He decides against re-reading his work so far, pushes the word processor back to the edge of the desk, takes a fresh white sheet of paper from the printer tray and writes at the top of the page in clear, blue ink. Chapter 10. He underlines it, leans back and raises his eyes to the ceiling. A pause, like a musical interval, and then he begins to write, the ink flowing smoothly from the nib in broad, deliberate strokes, the words chosen in full awareness, his mind as clear as a morning sky.

After a few hundred words, he puts down the pen and rummages through a box on the floor. He brings out an old pipe of Frank's, scrapes a small amount of tobacco from around the hollow and pats it down again, tries to light it. It sputters and will not catch, but he keeps trying, holding matches at their very ends until the flames burn his fingers. Eventually the tobacco filings light and the familiar smell rises. Martin breathes him in, and coughs. *It wouldn't have been long before you bought a bloody pipe.* He laughs at himself, grips the hard stem between his teeth and begins to write again.

Before he has finished another page, something occurs to him. He checks the title written neatly in pencil at the top of the original manuscript: *The Cry of All.* Something reverberates in his memory like a finger softly ringing round the edge of a glass. Martin reaches for his dictionary of quotations and looks for the words 'the game of the few': he's found them here once before. He looks up under 'game' and there it is, BERK 65:9, George Berkeley 1685–1753, Irish philosopher and Anglican bishop. *Truth is the cry of all, but the game of the few.* Siris (1744) para. 368. Martin swallows hard. He takes up the pen and writes.

He's coming to the end when the phone rings. It's Alice.

'Am I disturbing you? I just wanted to check on Lance.'

'He's fine. We're both fine.'

'Good. Good. So how's it going then?'

'The book? I'm just finishing the final chapter.'

'That's great, Martin. I can't wait to read it.'

'Just the epilogue to go now.'

'Great.'

'What are you doing?'

'Oh, nothing much, having a lazy night.'

'Do you want to come around for a drink?'

'What, now?'

'Yeah. Only if you want to.'

'Um, okay. If I wouldn't be taking you away from your work.'

'I'm finished for tonight anyway.'

'Okay, I'll see you soon then.'

'Alice...'
'Yes?'
'I'm sorry.'

He goes back to the study, writes the last few lines and tucks the finished pages away in a folder. Only the epilogue to go. Martin feels inexplicably sad. He busies himself tidying the desk. Alice would never believe he could have become so slovenly: there are sprawling piles of papers, cards all out of order. Perhaps he needed to lose control a bit. He picks out a scrap of paper from under the blotter.

The ferment of genius, Holmes said, is quickly imported and when a man is great he makes others believe in greatness. By that token one's life is altered. One has climbed a hill, looked out and over and the valley of one's own condition will be forever greener.

Genius. It turns out Frank is no genius. Frank isn't even great. Martin has come to know not greatness, but the flaws hidden within. And within himself. His life is indeed altered.

He goes to answer the doorbell. It's Alice. They are strangely shy with each other. She comes in as if it is not her house, waits to be shown where to sit, like a guest. He offers her a drink.

'Cognac, thanks.'

As if he doesn't know what she drinks.

'Lance is asleep if you want to go check on him.'

'I'm sure he's fine.'

Martin's relieved at her trust.

'So, if you've nearly finished the book, you must have decided what to do about Frank.'

'Ye-es.'

'What have you decided to do?'

'I went to see Connie.'

There's a pause. It feels good to talk to Alice, to have her sitting opposite him on the couch, feet tucked up under her as usual, nodding in that way of hers. He loves her.

'We talked about it rather indirectly, but it was clear she would refuse to admit any of it. She called it an act of love.'

'And so you are keeping the secret?'

'I . . . I think so.'

'That would be a kind of act of love too, wouldn't it?'

He says nothing.

'You've changed, Martin. I can see it.'

He picks at his fingernails, nods, without looking up.

'I feel like . . . only now am I coming back to my world.' He raises his eyes to hers, trembles a little. 'It sounds ridiculous, but I feel like I've been *transformed*.'

Alice moves over to sit next to him, puts an arm around his shoulder and pulls his head down towards hers, like a large bird gathering her young under a wing. He feels safe there, holds her, nuzzles her neck gently. She strokes his hair.

'I've been looking for the truth so long, and then I didn't know what to do when I found it. It almost seems a betrayal simply to cover it up again, run away.'

'Some truths are better left lying undisturbed.'

'The more I think of it –' he jerks his head upwards, pulls away from her to look her squarely in the face, 'the more I ask myself, are our lives untrue? Are our most basic beliefs about ourselves wrong?'

'And how do you answer?'

'I think sometimes we are absolutely blind to the fundamentals. I know I have been.'

He is surprised to feel a teardrop sliding down his cheek. They stay sitting on the couch, holding each other, for a long time.

Martin doesn't want to go to the Te Papa seminar but he supposes he has to. The Assistant Dean rang up specifically to ask him, and he doesn't often ask for anything. He's hinted that Martin should start going to more university functions, that eyebrows are being raised that his sabbatical is being extended again. Everyone understood about Frank's death, of course, terrible, but you know how the department operates.

Martin knows all right. He knows he doesn't want to go back.

Still, he decides to attend the seminar. The topic looks marginally interesting: *The victim's identification with his executioner: Schreiber's seventh stage of culpabilisation.* It'll be interesting to swallow a piece of academia again. For a while there, under Frank's influence, he guesses, he found it all absurd; but now he almost misses it.

Martin hasn't been to the Museum of New Zealand much. With all its buttons and flashing lights it seems to him more like a kids' playground than a serious guardian of culture and history, and he has to ask the way to the seminar room. It's up the stairs, in a small white amphitheatre off to the left. He's running late, and the introduction has already begun. He finds an empty seat in the back row and sits, trying not to draw attention to himself. Collins has seen him anyway, and raises a finger in recognition. Martin looks around the audience and sees other familiar faces – lecturers, students. It seems he knew them all in another life.

It's some time before his mind concentrates on the address by the visiting professor. He really should have read more Schreiber. The professor is speaking of how Schreiber's friend Franz Blau mythologised the writer.

'Following Blau's example, there was a group of critics who examined the books of Schreiber exclusively within the micro-context of biography. Rather than consider the work within the context of literary history, this group followed a strictly biographical explanation, declaring Schreiber's books inseparable from his person. The hero of his novels therefore becomes none other than the author himself and the author's life becomes the key to the meaning of the work. Or, taken to extremes, the meaning of the work is as a key for understanding the biography. In the hands of such critics, Schreiber's biography becomes hagiography.'

The professor goes on to critically discuss the treatment of Schreiber, not as novelist, but as philosopher, and Martin's mind drifts away on a path from his earlier words. It's clear artistic works have more uses beyond keys to biography. But surely that's still a valid purpose? Not in isolation, perhaps, and not through misrepresentation. But how to be sure of your interpretation? He has certainly got it wrong with Frank. Or has he? What he's written already has its own truth to it. Out of all twelve texts, only one is proved false, and even that one's still substantially Frank. It isn't as if Connie's original manuscript hasn't been significantly altered. The criticisms of the text on the basis of the Finnigan trademarks – the exaggerated event, looping time structure, metaphor of weather and animals, themes of seeking escape from restriction, the futile struggle for lost dignity – all still hold true. He's taken the story and made it his own creature. Why should it not be analysed on that basis?

His biography can stand well as it is. There's no need to destroy everything with the revelation.

Martin listens to the rest of the address without hearing the words. He sits slumped, flooded with relief and exhaustion. At the end he goes up to Collins, to thank him for inviting him along.

'You enjoyed it then?'

'Absolutely.'

'I thought you would. He's a very passionate defender of the moral rights of the artist. Speaking of which, what is your opinion of the Finnigan exhibition next door? Does it capture him?'

Martin isn't sure what to say.

'Actually, I haven't seen it yet.'

'Martin! Good God, I'd have thought you'd have been the first one through the door.'

'I'd completely forgotten it was opening this week. Honestly. Too busy, you know. Do excuse me – I'll go have a look at it now.'

Martin makes his way through the loitering students to the door, but instead of turning off towards the exhibition he swerves into the side toilets. He feels suddenly faint. He hadn't forgotten. He just couldn't face it. Well, he'll have to go now. He sits down in a cubicle and puts his head between his knees, breathes in slowly, the sour smell of urine wrinkling his nose. He didn't have breakfast this morning; perhaps he just needs a strong coffee. He straightens slowly, stands and flushes, opens the door and goes to the sink to wash his hands. His face reflected in the mirror is oddly pale and he can see glimpses of himself as a young boy hidden in the folds of freshly shaved skin. He puts one hand up to the glass and traces the outline of his cheek. Someone's coming in. He hurriedly dries his hands and leaves.

The exhibition is in a narrow, elongated room, more like a large corridor than an enclosed box of walls. By the door is Anne Hessel's large oil portrait of Frank, his birdlike eyebrows brooding down on his audience, and a quote below: '*Fiction is, by definition, unfaithful. Reality cannot be recounted by writers, our purpose is rather to reinvent it*'.

Martin looks up at the oily grey eyes glaring at him, and glares back. He never did like that painting. He steps into the room and looks around. Only two other people are in there, peering into glass display cases. Along the back wall is a single shelf lined with every edition of Frank's works, even the translations, all different sizes and colours. Martin begins by walking alongside the texts, running his index finger over their spines, counting. There are eighty-eight. Fifty-seven are of *The Game of the Few*. In the corner a video of the film version is running on a television screen. It's up to the scene where Rex is walking with the countess through Red Square.

On the next wall are photos of Frank: Frank as a boy with his father; Frank in high school receiving an award; young Frank in his army uniform; Frank on a chain gang at a freezing works; Frank in Hong Kong; Frank the journalist in a Wellington newsroom; an older Frank puffing on his pipe at a desk piled high with books; Frank looking cranky; Frank and Connie together out on their deck on a sunny day, smiling. A small credit underneath: photos supplied by Constance Finnigan.

Martin wanders past the glass cases to the other side of the room. He sees under the glass the collection of letters, a few diaries, the partial manuscript. It feels like his own belongings on display.

On this side of the room is a picture of Frank speaking to a literary audience. Martin hears a whirring and a tape clicks on. It's the interview from the oral history archives, 1988. Martin sits, although he's heard it before. He closes his eyes and imagines Frank in his leather chair, that all-knowing look of his.

'I was forty-two years old before I had the courage to do what I really wanted to do – write fiction full-time. Fortunately I'm still doing it twenty years later and I expect I'll be doing it until I die.'

His familiar cackle-cough.

'You know I had to go into the government offices the other day to fill out a form about my superannuation, and the young bloke there, all pimply and straight out of school he was, asked me if my income was over a certain level, and I replied yes it was. Well, this fella looks surprised, says to me, "What, are you still working?"'

Cackle, splutter, cough, cough.

'I'm amazed at it myself. Amazed I can actually earn a living, I mean. You know, there was no support when I began writing, none of this Arts Council shit, pardon the language. Even when there was, it was full of complete no-hoper ning nongs. They became more enlightened, though. So enlightened, they eventually offered me some money. Not until after *The Game of the Few*, of course, not until I was already successful and didn't need their paltry $2000. They only gave me $2000, you know – 1973, that was – and I was considerably pissed off because Skidmore got $3000. I was fucking appalled. 'Scuse the language.'

Martin laughs aloud. He'd forgotten that bit.

'Speaking of *The Game of the Few*, tell me, did you ever think it would be so successful?'

'Well, yeah, I did know I had something pretty damn good there. I did know that, but you can never predict what will catch the wave of public opinion, you know, or what will just miss the crest and get swamped. I really had faith in that book, though – I did from the moment I first saw it, you know, envisioned it. I thought it was too ambitious initially, so I altered some of the direction as I went along, made it more accessible. But that book, you know, that idea, was a real gift. There's not a day still that I don't remind myself to acknowledge that.'

'Do you believe in God then?'

'God? (He chuckles.) No, not God. I believe in humanity, in the human spirit. That's what my books are all about.'

The tape clicks off but Martin continues to sit there. He's heard the interview before, knows its contents intimately, but he's never really heard the words. A gift? It was a gift all right.

He starts to laugh, a gentle, billowing sound, that builds to a great sheet of silent noise flapping against the walls. He laughs and laughs and laughs.

Martin goes into his study and looks at the last few pages scrawled the night before and lying on the desk. It's done. He picks them up and walks over to the armchair in the bay window, draws back the heavy curtain and sits. The bright morning sunlight speckles through a tree outside, dances lightly across the pages. He imagines the fragile sheets of paper in his lap are the delicate wings of a newly hatched butterfly just emerged from its dark chrysalis, drying its thin membranes in the sun. Soon it will spread its new wings and trust itself to the void.

Epilogue

A biographer has to adjust and weigh varying accounts of a person. He has to assume one person is lying, another misremembers, another has a vested interest. Somewhere in between you have to feel your way to reality, to a sense of the man.

My sense of Frank Finnigan has changed over time, as his own sense of self also changed. The sense and emotion attached to his memories altered, subtly, so the meanings of past events coloured in light of other events, to form rich paintings quite different from those initial sketches. I believe, even if he was not always aware of it, Frank enjoyed this process, which is not unlike that undergone in a novel. He was drawn to story telling, not so much because he was a liar, but because he delighted in the richness of the layers of colours tightly packed between the pages. His personal revisionism was echoed in a larger scale in the social revisionism found in his novels.

'Stories are less about facts and more about meanings,' he once said. And that is true also of his life. Together, Frank and I have woven together a collection of facts to form a life story here, a personal myth of memory. But memory is a construction, it is a fiction and, as such, has as much truth in it. I have come to understand that such truths are as real, if not more so, than others more tangible.

Frank initially did not want his biography to be written. When I first approached him in 1987, as a Masters graduate lecturing part time at the University of Canterbury, he declined. I won't say politely, because it wasn't. The reply was typically Frank. He argued that his works should stand for themselves. Ten years later, after the threat of an unauthorised biography, he changed his mind and asked me to write the approved version. Approved in that he would co-operate with me, give me access to letters, original manuscripts, suggest people I should talk to, spend many hours himself being interviewed. Frank never read this biography; unfortunately, he died before it was complete. I sometimes wonder if he would have demanded anything be changed. I like to believe he would have been happy with it as it is.

In this biography I spend much consideration on the question of whether the work and the life can be dissociated. I have analysed Finnigan's material to find the keys to the deeper side of my subject: the keys to the private mythology of the individual. I hoped that by revealing the patterns and modes of the man's works, I would reveal the man. This is the constant struggle between biographer and subject, the struggle between concealed and revealed, public and private. There are some aspects I deliberately chose not to reveal. While this has caused me some anguished internal debate, I have made the decisions I can live with.

I still believe the argument for reading the works critically informed by biography is a valid one, as by ascertaining the author's meaning of the symbols and myths used in the work, we decipher the symbolic code of imagery and metaphor. Emotions translated into images and symbols become biographical statements. However, I have perhaps changed my view on how much can be known, even by the author. I now have a better understanding of man's gift for altering experience in his imagination and thereby altering his concept of himself. I have a better understanding of self-deception.

The long journey I took with Frank has taught me many things. The more I got to know him, and to recognise his stubborn refusal of introspection, despite the intelligence and humanity to be found in his literature, the more I gained in self-knowledge. I may not be a better person for having written about his life, but I believe I am a wiser one.

Martin Wrightson, 1998

Epilogue

'So, what did you think?'

'Masterful,' said Alice.

'Really?'

'Absolutely. If that doesn't have them flocking to the bookstores I don't know what will.'

She switched the TV off by remote control.

'They better wait until after the launch next week. You are coming to it aren't you?'

'Of course. My clever husband.'

She stood up and stretched, smiling at him, then leant down and patted Martin on the knee.

'Just promise me you'll never write another one.'

'It's highly unlikely.'

He smiled back. He was rather pleased with the way the TV interview turned out. Dick Young had been a bit of a pillock but Martin thought he'd come across well, said all the things he wanted to say.

'I'm off for a bath and then bed. You coming?'

'Soon. I'll just tidy a few things up in the study.'

'Don't be long.'

Alice stretched again and yawned. Martin noticed a few strands of white hidden amongst her thick, shiny black hair. They were both getting older. How would they be when they were old? He thought of Frank, followed Alice into the hall and turned into his study where a proof copy of the book lay out on the desk. Done.

'So you knocked the bugger off at last, did you?'

Bloody did, Frank, bloody did.

Martin gathered the last corrections into a pile and wrapped a manila folder around them, slipped it into the top drawer of the desk. He would file them properly later; first, there was all this other crap to get rid of. It had been lying here for weeks, forgotten. He sorted out the rest of the jumbled papers into transcripts, background, historical, family and the other categories he had neatly labelled in his card catalogue at the very beginning, almost two years ago. His work habits had certainly deteriorated as he went along. But he didn't need such strict structures any more. He could let things find their own place. He gradually cleared the desk, a little sadly now, clearing away all signs of Frank, who he'd lived with for so long. What would the next project be? Perhaps some of his own fiction. He'd have a break first, settle back into the routine of university, the lectures and tutorials, the straightforward judgements of essays and exams. It'd be good to have some normalcy for a while. Just get settled back in. Then maybe he could write some stories.

'Do what you want to do. Just do it, kid. Don't talk about it, don't dream about it, don't put it off till you know what you're doing, or wait till you know what you want to say, just sit down and do it.'

Martin sat down at the desk, the puff gone out of him. He picked up a fountain pen, opened his writing pad. Some scribbled notes from an interview with Frank, he flicked forward, was stopped by two perfect circles nestled together in a worn figure of eight and his poem.

> *I walk this winding road for miles*
> *and soon it will be night.*
> *I trip and fall and fear that I*
> *may yet forsake this fight.*
> *Midway upon this journey*
> *I know not where I will*

> *each signpost has a question*
> *each turn another hill.*
> *I dare not stop and sit awhile*
> *I dare not ask you lest*
> *you tell me you are lost as well*
> *and I let go this quest.*

Martin blinked, the pen trembled. He sat for a minute, his eyes following the loops of the tiny black words over and over. Then he set the pen a few lines underneath, and wrote.

> *Then night does fall and all is black*
> *I close my eyes to sleep*
> *Fear of nightmare stems my slumber*
> *and as I sow, I reap.*
> *Surely as the sun must rise,*
> *darkness must break its veil.*
> *Then awake the dawn's first rays*
> *and so, I shall not fail.*
> *The sun appears, its light so clear*
> *like past days once enjoyed*
> *I must stand, open my wings, trust*
> *myself into the void.*

Martin blinked again, set the pen down. He stood up and went to the door, switched off the light, then looked back. He imagined, in the shadows around the desk, Frank sitting heavily down on the chair, picking up the paper and reading.

'Load of bloody bollocks.'

Martin smiled and quietly shut the door behind him.